THE SECRET OF SANCTUARY

Samantha Wolf Mysteries

Book 11

TARA ELLIS

THE SECRET OF SANCTUARY
ISBN: 9781097886241

Model: Breanna Dahl
Photographer: Tara Ellis Photography

NOTE FROM THE AUTHOR

This particular story was a special project for me because for the first time, I was able to create a cross-over with my other series. You see, I also write an adult cozy mystery series under the pen name of Tara Meyers, called The Secrets of Sanctuary Cozy Mysteries. Why the different name? Only because of marketing reasons. I keep my children and adult platforms separate for advertising, but they are both clean reads. It's been so much fun to have Ember Burns and other characters from the town of Sanctuary in Sam's world! I knew the two would go well together. I hope you agree, and get as much fun out of solving the mystery as I did writing it!

SAMANTHA WOLF MYSTERIES

1. The Mystery of Hollow Inn
2. The Secret of Camp Whispering Pines
3. The Beach House Mystery
4. The Heiress of Covington Ranch
5. The Haunting of Eagle Creek Middle School
6. A Mysterious Christmas on Orcas Island
7. The Case of the Curious Canine
8. The Legend of Shadow Mountain
9. The Mystery of Old Gully Trail
10. Return to Hollow Inn
11. The Secret of Sanctuary

Find these and Tara's other titles on her author page at Amazon!

CONTENTS

1

ON THE ROAD AGAIN

"I'm pretty sure that ollygander is *not* a word." Cassy leans back in the booth and folds her arms over her chest. Staring across at Hunter, she ignores his big brown puppy eyes and points a finger at him, narrowing her own eyes. "I challenge it."

Throwing his hands up in the air, Hunter issues a dramatic sigh. "Fine," he hollers, looking over his shoulder and toward the front of the motorhome. "Lisa!"

Lisa Covington, Cassy's older sister, glances up in the large rearview mirror. But only briefly. While she's used to hauling horse trailers around, as special as the horses are, the five young teens seated at the table are very special cargo. "Lay it on me!"

"Ollygander," Hunter says smugly. "You know, it's when you linger while looking at something."

Shaking her blonde head, Lisa snorts loudly. "Nice try, Hunter. I'll give you points for creativity, but that's it. I don't have to be a teacher to call foul on that one."

Samantha Wolf rolls her eyes at her brother's antics in response to the denial. They both have the dark hair of their father, but Sam's eyes are an unusual shade of green. At fifteen, Hunter is two years older than she is, but sometimes she swears he's only ten. She doesn't know how Lisa can be so patient with him. Maybe being a teacher at the middle school she and her girlfriends go to has something to do with that.

"Earth to Sam."

Sam focuses on her best friend, Allyson Parker. She's seated in between her and Cassy, while Hunter and Lisa's older brother, John, are across from them. The large motorhome accommodates a horseshoe-shaped table that seats six instead of the more standard four. Sam's dog, Rocky, is taking up the extra space at the head of the table.

"Sorry, Ally," Sam replies with a crooked grin. Chewing on her bottom lip, she pushes her overgrown bangs out of her eyes and stares at the game tiles. It doesn't help. She still has horrible letters. "Ugh," she mumbles. Plucking two tiles off her rack, she uses an existing E to spell 'the'.

"Really?" Hunter laughs. "You may as well just quit now before this gets too embarrassing."

Ally puts a restraining arm around Sam's shoulders. They're only two hours into their week-long summer vacation and it's already looking like World War Three. Hunter's on a roll, and he knows exactly how to push Sam's buttons. Ally has witnessed it countless times before and she doesn't want this trip to get off on the wrong foot. "Maybe we should play something else."

Cassy leans in closer to Ally and peeks at her tiles. "Nah," she whispers. "We can't give up now. Look, you've got a killer word."

"Hey!" Hunter scolds. "You can't help each other. Ouch!" Rubbing at his shoulder, he glares at John. The older boy is also much larger than him.

"Leave 'em alone, Hunter. Don't be a sore loser." John's bright-blue eyes scrunch up as he smiles good-naturedly at his best friend. Although seventeen and two years ahead of Hunter in high school, they still spend most of their free time together. His blonde hair is a stark contrast to Ally's red, but the siblings have a lot of other similarities.

Sam reaches up and gives Ally's hand on her shoulder a reassuring squeeze. She understands her friend's wariness. Sam's spent nearly as much time being grounded due to the epic fights with Hunter, as she has from the trouble her and Ally have gotten into from chasing after mysteries. But she knows how much everyone is looking forward to this camping trip, including her.

"Hunter's right," Sam states cheerfully. She's greeted with open-mouthed stares. And silence. Lot's of silence. "We're thirteen now, girls. We can come up with our own words. Besides," she adds with a wink, "there's three of us and two of them. Hardly a fair match-up."

Hunter covers his shock with a classic deflection. "If you want to make this girls against boys, I don't have a problem with that. John and I can easily take you all on."

John runs his hands through his slightly overgrown hair before pointing at his sister. "Ally, just put down whatever word you want. It doesn't matter."

"Are we there yet?" Hunter calls out, already forgetting about the battle of the sexes.

"We're twenty minutes closer than the last time you asked," Lisa replies pleasantly. "We should be at Sanctuary campground in an hour, but I'm going to stop in town first to get some fuel."

"Snacks." Cassy slips under the table. After pushing her way through the multitude of legs, she pops out the other side. "We need snacks."

Rocky barks in support of the announcement. The cinnamon-colored poodle has what's called a teddy bear cut, which makes him look like a stuffed animal. Hunter lovingly calls him Chewbacca. But he's Sam's shadow and has been ever since she adopted him from the animal shelter she and the girls volunteered at the year before.

"Rocky agrees," Hunter laughs. "Oh! And

drinks. I put some extra soda in the fridge before we left. And a package of beef jerky in the cupboard."

Smiling broadly, Cassy starts collecting items and piling them around the gameboard, her conflict with Hunter forgotten. There wasn't anything a good snack binge between them couldn't smooth over.

Sam has no idea where her friend puts all the food. Sam is the tallest of the three girls, but Cassy's a close second. And where Ally is slender, the other two have more of an athletic build. However, when it comes to eating, Cassy can run circles around them both.

Tugging at her long, jet-black hair that's pulled back in a ponytail, Cassy's face grows serious. Pausing before ducking back under the table, her brows furrow. "I'm super excited about our week-long camping trip, but I hope Penny and her parents can manage the horses okay. It's not like they can call us if they have a problem."

"Penny's going to do fine," John assures her.

Penny is a young girl who lives down the hill from Covington Ranch, where Cassy and Lisa live. They'd recently become friends with Penny and she was helping with horse riding classes at the ranch over the summer.

"Besides," Sam adds, "her parents will be overseeing everything, and all they have to do is feed the horses and muck some stalls. Lisa said she can use the park phone to check in daily." While the Sanctuary campground didn't have WiFi or cellphone coverage, it did have a regular phone in the office that could be used by guests.

Sam looks out the large window next to the table and admires the passing scenery. They're already deep in the mountains of the Cascades, in Washington State. They live in a small ocean town and are used to the dramatic beauty of the state, but the thick woods and craggy mountains always take Sam's breath away. She wishes they could open the window and let in the sweet scent of pine needles.

"Yes!"

Re-focusing on Cassy, she sees her friend has set out an impressive word. Instead of pouting, Hunter nods in appreciation, causing Sam to smile. For all the bantering, they're all very good friends, and she has no doubt the next week will be full of the usual fun. Her smile wavering, she turns back to the blurred scenery, the skin along the back of her neck prickling. She has a habit of finding a mystery in the most unlikely places, and she has a strong feeling Sanctuary isn't going to be any different.

2

FINDING SANCTUARY

"Nature's Brew." Ally squints up at the quaint wooden sign while reading the name of the coffee shop out loud. "Looks like a cute place."

Sam nods in agreement before ducking in through the door Cassy's holding open for them. Lisa is already inside, eagerly waiting in line to order what is sure to be a potent, caffeinated drink. The boys opted to stay back at the gas station with the motorhome, so long as they promised to bring them something.

"Hunter wants an Italian soda," Cassy announces, hands on hips. "I think I'll try one, too. Raspberry sounds good."

Sam scrunches up her nose. Spending five dollars of her hard-earned allowance on a drink isn't something to take lightly. While both of her friends have a larger cash flow, her family lives on a more limited budget. Her mom quit her teaching job three years ago to stay home after her twin sisters where born. Her father has a good job heading up several fishing operations in Alaska, but there still isn't much extra. Sam has learned over the years to budget and right now, the forty dollars she has in her pocket doesn't seem like a lot. Lisa's being very generous and covering all the regular costs, including food, but for anything extra like souvenirs and expensive, sugary drinks, they're on their own.

"Do you want to split one?" Ally offers. "I don't think I can drink one on my own."

Sam smiles gratefully at her best friend. She and Ally have practically grown up together and no one understands her better. "Thanks, Ally. But get whatever flavor *you* want."

After giving Ally some money, Sam wanders around the small shop to browse all of the souvenirs. She wished the sweatshirts weren't so much. Even though it was early July and sure to be hot the whole week, it would still be nice to have at night around the campfire. The old one she brought would have to do.

Finding herself at the large, storefront window, Sam looks out at the scenic town of Sanctuary. The small collection of buildings is nestled at the bottom of a valley. The mountains that surround it rise sharply toward a deep-blue sky, its snow-covered, jagged peaks glowing starkly against it. Thick woods that blanket the Cascades spread out into the valley, stopping only where the settlers cleared the land over a hundred years ago to plant their crops. According to Lisa's description as they'd approached the town, it was originally founded by loggers but now survives primarily off cattle and tourism.

Main Street could be a postcard for any historic western setting. In fact, Sam expects to see a horse come trotting up the street, or even a carriage. There are plenty of what you'd call 'cowboys' roaming about and Sam doesn't doubt most of them are residents, versus tourists paying dress-up.

You can tell by the worn boots.

Sam confirms her theory by studying the footwear of the nearest Stetson-wearing man on the wooden boardwalk passing the window. Sure enough, his leather boots are worn, scuffed and have their fair share of caked-on mud. Grinning, Sam looks across the street at two other men exiting a store. In contrast, their boots look brand new. Eyebrows pulling together, she also notes the clean blue jeans and bright flannel shirts. Not locals. Both men appear to be in their late twenties. Considering their overgrown hair and scruffy faces it strikes Sam that while they aren't well groomed, they're going out of their way to appear so. The taller of the two looks furtively around before grabbing the other man roughly by the arm and shoving him forward, toward the road. Yanking his arm away, the smaller man jams his hands into his pockets and stomps away, his face twisted with anger.

"Sam."

Sam jumps at her name and then laughs as she turns to face Lisa, who has a distinctly teacher-like expression. Sam squirms slightly under the scrutiny.

"I recognize that look on your face," Lisa

states while wagging a finger at Sam.

"But, I—"

"Uh-uh," Lisa interrupts. "Nope. We talked about this when our trip was first planned so you go right ahead and ignore any unusual, suspicious, or out-of-place anomaly. Got it?" Although completely serious, Lisa is still smiling. Sam might manage to get herself into some crazy situations, but the intent is always good.

Unable to come up with an honest reply, Sam simply accepts the scolding and nods once before shuffling over to stand with Ally. Her friend is currently trying to place their order, but the barista is making things difficult.

"Are you sure you want something so boring?" The petite woman leans forward on the counter, widening her eyes as she speaks. "How about a Rodeo King Cowboy Mudslinger? It's got enough chocolate to hype you up for half the day."

Laughing, Ally gives her red curls a quick shake. "No, thank you. Just an orange Italian Soda."

Slapping her hands on the counter dramatically, the barista feigns defeat. "Okay. I guess if I was going for something plain, I'd get that, too." Winking once, she turns to gather the needed ingredients.

"I'll be waiting out front, girls!" Lisa calls to them as the bell over the opening door dings.

"You're with the Grande, super skinny, whammy, plain cow?"

Sam and Ally simply stare at the girl behind the counter. Cassy snorts from beside them, where she's been slurping down her own raspberry-flavored drink.

Chuckling, the barista adds ice to the soda and orange syrup. According to her large, elaborately decorated nametag, her name is Mel. "That's what I call a twenty ounce, no fat, four shot vanilla latte.

"That's Lisa, my sister" Cassy explains, moving up to the counter.

"And our teacher, Miss Covington," Ally adds.

"Sounds confusing." Sliding the finished drink across the counter, Mel looks amused. "That'll be four fifty."

Sam figures Mel must be in her mid-twenties, close to Lisa's age. Her long, jet-black hair is in braids, making her appear younger. The mischievous glint in her eyes leaves no doubt that she's always upbeat and playful. "It used to be when we first met Lisa and became friends with Cassy," Sam agrees. "But now it's just second nature not to use her first name at school."

Ally hands Mel a five-dollar bill. "Please, keep the change."

Grinning a thanks, Mel finishes the transaction. "Lisa told me you're staying in the Sanctuary campground. It should be an interesting week to be there."

Sam pauses mid-sip. "What do you mean?"

Hesitating, Mel then glances around before leaning forward conspiratorially. "Let's just say you have a good chance of encountering some… ancient secrets."

3

UNEARTHING THE PAST

It takes all of Sam's willpower to not discuss Mel's mysterious comment the whole half-hour to the campground. Especially considering Lisa's recent warning. Unfortunately, Cassy isn't as compelled and told the boys as soon as they reached the motorhome.

"You've been unusually quiet," John says while eyeing Sam suspiciously.

They've just pulled off the main road and are headed farther into the woods, following the brown, wooden signs for Sanctuary campground. Although the area is a popular spot for outdoor enthusiasts, Lisa promised this was one of the more remote campsites. They passed a gorgeous lake a few miles back, which is on the itinerary for tomorrow. The week is already planned out with a guided hike to some waterfalls, swimming at the lake, a day at the town of Sanctuary to attend a rodeo, and plenty of free time to explore the woods, sit around the campfire, and play the multitude of games they brought.

Sam pushes thoughts of the week aside to address John's question. It's not a simple answer. She wants to be honest but also avoid any further accusations of intentionally looking for trouble. John has a way of making her feel guilty before she's even had a chance to earn the blame. Probably because he's usually right. "I want this to be a fun week. I'll just worry Lisa if I go on about a mystery at the campground before we even get there. That'd be a record, even for me."

Snorting, John then nods approvingly. "Good call. Nothing but smore's and mosquito bites on the agenda."

Two quick blasts of the horn interrupt their conversation, followed by whoops of joy by Hunter. Looking out the window next to her, Sam can see they're driving under a large, lodgepole sign.

"We're here!" Lisa calls out happily, tapping the horn one more time. "I'm going to go inside the office and confirm the spot and get a map of the campground. Why don't you kids make a call to your parents and let them know we made it here safely?"

The smell of fresh pine and earthy loam greet them as they all clamber down the motorhome steps. They're officially on the eastern side of the Cascades, leaving behind the moss and thick undergrowth of ferns they're used to. Here, the ground is more sparsely covered with huge cedars and some other evergreens. Dry pine needles and pine cones litter the ground, interspersed with fallen trees and small shrubbery.

The paved parking lot is surprisingly vacant, with only two other trailers and a park ranger vehicle out in front of the log-cabin style building. The one road leading from the lot enters the woods and disappears from sight, leaving them to feel as if they're in some remote mountains, versus a state campground.

Rocky dashes past Sam's legs before she can grab him and begins barking at some unseen adversary amongst the trees.

"Rocky!" Sam hollers, chasing after him. While pets are welcome there, it was made clear on the website that they're expected to be leashed when out in public areas.

The poodle positions himself at the base of a nearby tree, obviously proud of the squirrel clambering up the trunk. Rocky, the mighty squirrel hunter.

Ally appears at Sam's side with a leash and doggy bag. "Here. Thought you might need these."

Sam smiles a crooked grin. "Thanks." Clipping the leash onto Rocky's collar, she does her best to drag him away from his prisoner. "Come on, Rocky! Let's go potty." Leading him over to a large grassy area, she then squints up at the sun. It's a hot day, even this high in the mountains.

"I've successfully convinced mom we're unharmed," Hunter announces somewhat smugly. Tossing a piece of licorice at Cassy, he sticks a new one into his own mouth. "They have snacks for sale!" he says around the candy.

Cassy hops up and down briefly before

taking a bite. "Perfect. I hope our spot isn't too far away."

Rolling her eyes, Sam leads Rocky back to the motorhome. "Great," she mutters to John in passing. "Like the two of them aren't hyper enough already."

"Hello there!"

Turning toward the source of the voice, Sam finds herself facing a man around thirty in a park ranger uniform. He has sharp, angular features and jet-black hair. But while Cassy's dark characteristics come from her Hispanic heritage, the ranger is obviously Native American. Though his eyes are friendly, he's pointing at Rocky. "I'm sorry!" Sam blurts. "He ran out before I could get his leash on, but I promise to be more careful. I cleaned up after him," she adds desperately, afraid again of being a source of trouble for the trip.

"I was going to thank you for having him on a leash," the ranger says pleasantly. "Most people ignore the signs. What's his name?"

"Rocky," Sam says with relief. "He's really very friendly."

"I'm sure he is." Petting Rocky's head, the

man turns to address the rest of the kids. "Staying in the campground?"

"Yes, sir," John answers. "For the whole week."

"My sister is inside, checking us in," Cassy offers.

"You've picked a good week. My name is Nathan Sparks," he says, holding a hand out first to John. "This is one of the many campgrounds I patrol."

They each introduce themselves, ending with Sam. Nathan's grip is firm, and his easy-going personality immediately puts Sam at ease. "Why is it a good week?"

Before Nathan can answer, a large, noisy truck pulls into the lot. It's hauling a trailer with the logo of a local state college on its side. Behind it are two other vehicles. By the way they follow the truck, it's clear they're all together.

Nathan nods at the procession. "I was going to say because of the amazing weather that's forecasted, but I imagine you might find that interesting, too."

As Sam watches, the middle-aged driver of the pickup goes to the back of the trailer and swings the doors open before disappearing inside. The nearest door pivots toward them on its hinges, and Sam can clearly see the words "Department of Archeology and Ancient Civilizations".

"Who are they?" Ally asks, curious now.

"A group of archeology students from the university," Nathan explains. "The state just approved a temporary dig permit for them."

"What kind of dig?" John takes a step in their direction, trying to get a look inside the trailer.

"Apparently, the professor discovered some sort of ancient mound. An effigy, I believe it's called. They're built by ancient people and are usually used for burials and contain other artifacts." Nathan scratches briefly at his jaw while peering in the direction of the group. "That's what the state said, anyway. All I know is our campground is the closest to the site and they'll be here for most of the summer. They started setting things up this past weekend. Maybe they'll give you a tour. If you're into that sort of thing."

Sam's stomach does a small flip of excitement. An archeological dig! "Ancient secrets," she mumbles. *That's* what Mel was talking about. Her eyes wide, Sam catches Ally staring at her. The two friends exchange a knowing look. Their camping trip just got a whole lot more interesting.

4

GOOD INTENTIONS

"According to this, our spot should be right around this bend." Lisa holds a map out to show John, who's hovering at her shoulder.

"Ranger Sparks said it's the last one on the road and one of the biggest," John says, taking the map. "There!"

Lisa looks to where he's pointing and sees the marker with their number on it. Braking, she then carefully maneuvers the motorhome off the main road and onto the wide graveled pull-through spot. Coming to a stop she leans forward as far as she can to peer out the window. "Why don't a couple of you hop out and let me know when I'm lined up with the hook-ups. And make sure none of the slide-outs are going to hit a tree!" she adds, smiling as Sam and John rush to be the first two through the door.

Sam leaps to the ground and then pauses, taking in the view. Although they're in a large campground, she can only see a hint of the other trailers and tents near them. Their space is open, but it's surrounded by towering cedars. There's just enough foliage in between them and the other spots that there's a surprising amount of privacy.

John sprints around to the other side of the motorhome and locates the hookups before waving Lisa forward. Sam busies herself with making sure none of the slide outs line up with a tree. Once the large vehicle comes to a final stop, she joins John on the other side. With the view of the road effectively blocked, it really feels secluded. Smiling up at the towering evergreens, she takes in a deep breath of clean air while closing her eyes.

"Here's the water and electrical," John says as Lisa approaches. "I don't see any other hook-ups."

"That's because there aren't any," Lisa explains. "We were lucky to get this much. None of the sites have septic, so you may as well go find the nearest bathroom now!"

"I want to put our tent up first." Hunter tosses a bag at John, tent stakes gripped in his other hand.

Studying the rest of the space, Sam notices there are actually two large spots for tents on the far side of a rock-lined fire pit. A wooden picnic table is situated between the motorhome and the pit. Once they have all of their camp chairs out and organized it will be very comfy.

"Come on!" Cassy urges, pulling at Sam's arm. "The guys can get their tent up on their own."

Although the motorhome sleeps up to six, it was agreed early on that the boys would opt to have their own tent. Lisa has the only room, while the girls will sleep on the couch's pull-out bed. If they want more space, the table also converts into a smaller bunk.

"Yeah," Ally says, taking Sam's other arm. "First things first. I'm hoping the bathroom has showers!"

The three girls laugh together as they skip from the camping spot and down the road, arm in arm. The early afternoon sun is high above them, casting flickering shadows through the towering trees as a warm breeze stirs the branches.

Other vacationers wave as they pass, sharing a special camaraderie of enjoying the outdoors. Several fires are burning, permeating the park with the sweet smell of woodsmoke. It automatically creates a feeling of nostalgia for Sam, taking her back to numerous other camping trips she's been on with her family, growing up.

The nearest group of bathrooms aren't more than a couple of minutes away, with the men and women housed in two separate buildings. A large dumpster occupies the space between them, encased in a sturdy, metal container so as not to attract bears. A sign in front of it cautions campers not to leave any food out.

Sam's thankful they're in the motorhome, as she has a brief flashback to a terrifying encounter she had with a grizzly bear. There are only black bears in these mountains, which are much smaller and not as aggressive, but she still wants to do all she can to avoid them. "We'll need to make sure Hunter doesn't sneak any food into their tent."

Ally gives Sam a knowing smile. "Don't worry, John won't let him. Plus, I don't think *any* of us want to take a chance of facing off with another bear."

"This looks promising," Cassy observes as they approach the bathroom.

The grounds are well kept, and there are even signs in front of some of the bushes, explaining what they are. There's a tie down out front for leashed dogs, as well as a bench and cork-board for flyers and messages. A map of the campground is in the center of the board, with numerous trails outlined in red.

"Wow," Ally says. "We could spend most of the week hiking right here!"

As her outlook for their vacation continues to improve, Sam squeezes both Ally and Cassy's hands. "I'm so glad we were able to come! I'll bet there's warm showers, and look! According to this map, there's a swimming pool. Lisa didn't mention that. Good thing we brought our swimsuits for the lake."

Ally leads the way inside, letting out a squeal

of delight when she spots a row of showers. Clapping her hands, she rushes to inspect them, Cassy in tow. While Sam will admit she's also glad about the showers, she certainly isn't excited. Rinsing off in the lake would accomplish the same thing. Of course, she also didn't wear much make-up other than lip gloss and has been accused of not having any fashion sense.

Scrunching her nose up at the thought of comparing her wardrobe with her two friends, Sam turns in the opposite direction. She *does* like to have clean hands. Approaching a long counter with several sinks, she reaches to turn the water on the nearest one when a sound stops her.

It sounds like someone crying!

Turning away, her dirty hands forgotten, Sam heads for the source of the loud sobs. In front of the farthest and largest stall, she stops. "Hello? Are you okay?"

The crying immediately stops, followed by an odd choking sound as the girl on the other side of the door stifles her emotions. After a moment, she blows her nose but doesn't answer.

Sam shifts awkwardly from foot to foot as the silence draws out. She can hear Ally and

Cassy from the other side of the room, and their voices grow louder when they start in her direction. Leaning closer to the stall, she tries one more time, speaking discreetly. "Can I help you?"

"Why don't you mind your own business!"

Flinching like she's been slapped, Sam steps back, almost colliding with Ally who's walked up behind her. Raising her eyebrows questioningly at Sam, it's obvious her friend overheard the exchange.

"Sorry," Sam offers weakly before gesturing for Ally and Cassy to follow her outside.

"What was that all about?" Cassy asks once they're back in the sunlit afternoon.

Sam grimaces, already replaying the retort in her head. Had she been wrong to pry? But what if the girl really had needed help? "I heard her crying pretty hard so I just asked her if she was okay."

"Well, she didn't sound that young," Ally says, taking Sam's arm. She knows how sensitive her friend is when it comes to hurting others feelings, or overstepping boundaries whether it's intended or not.

"Well, I think she was rude," Cassy says with

a turn of her nose. "Forget about it."

"Why don't we go back and help get the camp situated, and then we can all go swimming," Ally suggests as they begin their trek back to the campsite.

Making an effort to smile, Sam nods in agreement. "That's a great idea. John and Hunter are going to be excited to find out about the pool!"

Their moods once again positive, the three friends head back out onto the road. After only a short distance, Sam can't help but look back. It's just in time to see movement near the bathrooms. Disappearing around the corner is a tall girl in her late teens, but other than a flash of khakis, all she sees is mass of long, black curls.

5

EFFIGY

Sam emerges from the motorhome towel-drying her hair. A couple of hours spent cooling off in the pool was exactly what they'd all needed. Now, having filled up on a quick sandwich she's ready to sit around the fire.

John already has one roaring in the pit, and Hunter is busy feeding it more wood. "We're going to run out pretty fast," he says while tossing on another piece.

"I remember seeing a truck near the entrance with a sign for firewood," Ally says thoughtfully as she plops into one of the camp chairs. Her red hair is piled up on top of her head in a messy bun, wild strands sticking out in various directions. She is fully embracing the whole natural thing.

"You all can go haul firewood if you want, but my legs are toast." Cassy takes the chair closest to Ally. Propping her feet up on a nearby rock, she begins massaging her calves. "I knew I shouldn't have caved to that final race."

"It wasn't even close," Hunter immediately responds.

John raises an eyebrow before snickering. "Sure, Hunter. Whatever you say." Slapping his friend playfully on the back he then turns to Lisa, who's already relaxing in a lounge chair. "Want me to go scope out the firewood situation?"

Giving a silent salute, Lisa smiles without opening her eyes. It's been a long day.

Sam calls Rocky over to join them on the quest for wood but frowns when she notices he's favoring one of his front paws. Kneeling down, she examines the pad and doesn't see anything obvious, but doesn't want to risk making it worse. "Cassy, can you keep an eye on Rocky? I think maybe he stepped on something."

Cassy silently sticks out a hand for the leash and then rests the other one gently on the poodle's head when he lies next to her chair.

As John heads for the road, he stops short when he sees another man approaching. Clad in a khaki outfit, he's loaded down with two backpacks, a leather satchel, a folded tarp stuck under one arm, and a duffel bag.

"Hello!" John calls out.

The middle-aged man pauses and glances in their direction. His face is scruffy with several days of growth, and it's clear he's doing his best not scowl at the interruption. "Hello."

Though not exactly an invitation to start a conversation, John takes a step toward him and extends a hand. "My name is John Parker. You must be with the archeology students?"

Sam peeks around John's back to get a better look at the man. The blue duffle bag is stamped with the same department name as the one on the trailer. She doesn't know much about college and stuff, but he looks a little old to be a student.

Accepting his fate, the man drops part of his load on the ground and forces a smile at John. Leaning forward, he takes John's hand in a firm shake. "Professor Tisdale," he says, emphasizing the word professor.

"Oh!" John's grin widens. "Are you in charge of the dig? I hate to impose, and I know you're busy, but do you think I could see the site sometime? I'm considering studying archeology in college."

His demeanor changing, Professor Tisdale's eyes brighten. "That's great! It's an amazing topic. Of course, I'm biased. You're welcome to observe our work whenever you'd like. In fact," he continues, nodding to the rest of the kids, "you can join me now if it's convenient. I'm on my way there."

Sam's need for the relaxing fire is quickly replaced with her desire for the offered adventure. *A real archeological dig!* "I'd love to go!" she blurts, then covers her mouth in embarrassment.

"You're all welcome," Professor Tisdale answers, chuckling at Sam's enthusiasm.

John looks back at Lisa for permission. She's opened her eyes and is clearly listening to the exchange. "I think it's a great idea. It's not often you get a chance to learn something while on vacation. I think I'll stay here and tend the fire. Rocky can keep me company."

Cassy jumps up, forgetting her aching legs. Ally glances up at her in surprise. "What? I got my second wind."

Smiling, Ally takes the hand Cassy holds out and allows herself to be pulled to her feet. Catching up quickly to Sam, who's already begun walking, she loops an arm through hers and gives a slight tug. When Sam turns a questioning look at her, she gives an exasperated chortle. "Samantha Wolf in the woods at some ancient artifact dig. What could possibly go wrong?"

Laughing, Sam pulls Ally along with her as Cassy joins them. "What sort of stuff do you think they're digging for?"

"Probably dinosaurs!" Hunter jeers as he jogs by, waving his hands in front of his chest like small arms. "Maybe a T-Rex."

Cassy laughs, but Sam rolls her eyes at her brother. "Not unless the T-Rex is a social creature."

Hunter makes a pitiful attempt at a growl as he reaches John. "What do you mean?"

"The name on the trailer?" When Hunter stares at Sam with a blank look, she continues with a triumphant air. "The Department of

Archeology and Ancient Civilizations. My guess is it's some sort of old village site."

Professor Tisdale nods in approval. "Good deduction, Miss –"

"Sam. Samantha Wolf."

"Good deduction, Samantha. While it's not a village, it *is* a remnant of an ancient people."

"Lucky guess," Hunter mutters.

Grunting as he hefts one of the bags back onto his shoulder, the professor eyes Hunter. "Brother?"

Hunter gives a crooked grin. "Hunter Wolf," he offers, confirming the shared last name with Sam.

Each of the kids go through a formal introduction, and Professor Tisdale graciously makes small talk with each of them before gathering the rest of his things.

"Let us help you," John offers, reaching for one of the backpacks.

Hesitating, Professor Tisdale then relinquishes the pack and nods in thanks as Hunter takes the satchel, and Sam the tarp. "That will make the trek a little easier."

"Are you sure it's okay for us to tag along?"

John asks. "We don't want to be a bother. I'm sure you're very busy."

"I'm a teacher," Professor Tisdale scoffs. Pointing to a marked trail not far past their campsite, he leads the way into the undergrowth. "I never pass up an opportunity to teach."

"What sort of remnant is it?" Sam asks while scurrying to be second in line behind John on the overgrown trail.

Without turning around, the professor clears his throat before entering what sounds like a lecture given a few times before. "We've discovered what's referred to as an effigy, or an effigy mound. Constructed mostly of dirt and some clay, we've so far dated it to the Woodland Period, about 2,000 years ago. It was most likely built by local Native Americans, or perhaps even some unknown indigenous peoples of the Americas."

"So, it's like a hill or something?" Hunter asks.

Making a chortling sound that Sam is quickly coming to recognize as the professor's sound of disdain, the older man stops and turns to address her brother. "Young man, it is *much* more than a 'hill'. It has the potential of being one of the more significant archeological finds of the year… possibly even the decade if what I suspect pans out as truth."

"Why is that, Professor?" John asks.

"Because until now, these mounds have never been found this far west. We've only just started our excavation and already we've uncovered some artifacts that hint at some shocking revelations regarding the peoples of the Woodland era. As far as social anthropology goes, this may very well be the holy grail."

"I'm surprised it isn't a bigger project, then," Sam observes. When the professor turns curious eyes in her direction, she's compelled to explain. "I mean, I just thought that if it were so important, there'd be a bunch more people and equipment out here."

Professor Tisdale turns back to the trail and begins again at a more rapid pace. "Unfortunately, Sam, archeology isn't as glamorous as the movies portray it. Rumors of this effigy have circulated this area for nearly a hundred years, since it was first discovered by some settlers. Over time, the location was lost and it became the thing of legends. It was only the last three years that there's been any sort of formal search for it. Thanks to a permit by the state to fly a specialized drone, we were able to do some specific topography passes and happened upon it. It was luck, really."

They walk in silence for several minutes. Just as Sam thinks the professor is done, he continues with a better explanation. "Even so, it took months for me to achieve the proper paperwork and licensure to conduct the dig. Then, I had to convince the college to back it. There was a lot of skepticism among my peers as to the validity of the mound. It wasn't until I was able to get everything on site and do my preliminary observations that I realized what we really have. I have yet to submit my most recent work, but once I do…"

Stopping again, Professor Tisdale holds his arms wide and then claps his hands together as he spins to face them. "I will finally achieve the recognition this find deserves. I hope to expand the license. As it stands, it's only for the summer and includes myself and five students. Hardly sufficient."

"How big is the effigy?" Ally asks when they begin hiking again. The terrain has begun to steepen, and the going is much harder than when they started.

"This one is small by comparison to some of the most well-known," Professor Tisdale answers. "It's three feet high at its tallest, ten feet wide and fifty feet long."

"I don't really understand," Cassy admits. "What is it?"

"Good question, Cassy," the professor praises. "The general consensus is that they were built primarily for spiritual purposes. Some, along with artifacts, contain burials of suspected higher placed people in their community."

Sam almost wishes Cassy hadn't asked. The idea of an ancient graveyard in the woods is spooky, even for her. Turning to glance back at Ally, the two share a look that confirms Ally is having the same thought. They all hike in silence for another ten minutes before the sound of a heated conversation reaches them from up ahead.

Pausing, Professor Tisdale calls out in a loud voice. "Hello!"

The voices stop and there's a moment of

stillness as the two groups get closer.

"I've got company," the professor continues in an authoritative tone. Pushing aside a branch, he steps out into a large opening cleared of trees, waving for the five kids to follow.

Close behind John, Sam steps around him once they're in the site. Professor Tisdale has already started the introductions, and Sam smiles in anticipation of meeting his team. However, once she spots the five students, the smile fades. Closest to her is a girl in her late teens, dressed in khakis, with a mass of distinctive black hair.

6

SITE UNSEEN

Sam does her best not to react. Maybe the girl didn't see them earlier when she came out of the bathroom. So long as Sam doesn't speak to her, she might be able to avoid causing an even more awkward situation.

"Cassy, what is your last name?" the professor is asking. He's got a remarkable memory and recited all of their names, except for Cassy.

"Covington," Cassy answers with a smile. "I don't think I told you what it was. Lisa, the woman back at the campground, is my sister."

Nodding as if it all makes sense now; Professor Tisdale turns his attention back to his students. "Isaac Moore is a third-year student and my right-hand man on this venture."

Isaac stands straighter with obvious pride, but his brows are furrowed in a deep scowl.

"I imagine he's also the source of the discourse we had the unpleasant misfortune to overhear." The professor crosses his arms and tilts his head, clearly waiting for an explanation.

Put on the spot in front of the young teens, Isaac's cheeks flush a deep red. "Mallory insists on challenging me when you're not around." Glaring at the dark-haired girl, it's obvious Isaac has more to say but thankfully chooses not to make a scene.

"The sign of a good leader is one who can be unsuccessfully challenged." Professor Tisdale silently looks from Isaac to the equally defiant girl. "Mallory Queen. A first-year student full of ambition. Let's do our best to keep it in check."

Mallory has the decency to look down at her feet before giving a slow nod but when she raises her eyes again, they rest squarely on Sam. Squinting slightly, she glances at Cassy and Ally before going back to Sam. "We've already met."

Sam squirms under the girl's intense gaze. In

normal circumstances, Mallory is someone Sam would want to get to know. There's a mysterious air about her. But it's clear she isn't interested in forming a friendship.

"Joseph Penn is my other first-year student," Professor Tisdale continues, saving Sam from any further discomfort.

Joseph looks up from where he's squatting next to a pile of loose dirt and gives a quick wave. He barely looks older than John.

"Candace Pulver and Greg Skinner are my second-year students and the rest of our team." Professor Tisdale skirts around an area staked out with string to join the last two students at a folding table. On it are two large wooden boxes topped with screens. The students appear to be sifting through the dirt and removing anything of interest. The professor holds up an item to the fading sun and gives a small grunt. Tossing it into the woods behind him, he then wipes his fingers on his pants. "As you can see, it's anything but glamorous, but this is what real archeological work is all about."

Sam steps up next to John to get a better look at the site. The larger trees are still in place, having grown right through the effigy, but all of the smaller trees and brush has been removed. With the undergrowth gone, the literal mound can be seen. An area of roughly ten feet out from the effigy is also cleared, giving room to walk and work around it. Sam can't help but be a little disappointed. It's basically a hill. The whole thing has been staked out and grids created by stretching and tying string to the wooden sticks. Three of the two-foot-square grids closest to them have been worked in, exposing around a foot of material. Sam wrinkles her nose. "Huh."

"Yeah." Cassy agrees with the sentiment. Elbowing Sam gently in the ribs, she points at the dirt. "Not exactly thrilling."

"Shhh," Ally hushes as she moves between the two girls. "Don't be rude."

"So, uh, you don't think there's any dinosaur bones in there?" Hunter asks.

John gives Hunter an exasperated look.

Joseph chuckles.

Mallory rolls her eyes.

"You seem to have an interest in paleontology," Professor Tisdale replies good-naturedly. "A very fascinating area of study, but you're off by several million years."

While Sam is normally the first to take an opportunity to tease her brother, she quickly intervenes. Hunter might make light of a lot of things, but he's actually quite smart and she doesn't want him to get defensive. "So, it looks like you've created different sections to dig stuff up," she interjects.

"We don't 'dig stuff up'," Mallory snaps. "It's a special process of excavation. We uncover the past and then decipher it."

"That sounds exciting," Sam says, trying again to be friendly.

Mallory snorts. "If you want exciting, go watch Indiana Jones. Archeology is a real science that involves a painfully long, precise process. One that if not done correctly can ruin everything." She certainly seems to be speaking to Sam, but Mallory is looking behind her while talking.

Giving up on forming a truce, Sam blinks twice before turning away from the rude girl and finds Isaac watching the exchange.

"Sorry." Standing, Isaac brushes his hands off on his pants before stepping carefully around the edge of the dig to join them. "It's been a long week and we're all a bit edgy. Where are you guys from?"

"Ocean Side," John answers. "It's a small town on the coast, about three hours from here."

Before they can engage in any further small talk, the unmistakable bray of a donkey echoes through the trees surrounding them. Her eyes widening in disbelief, Sam watches as a mule emerges from the trail. Riding him is an old, weathered man and an impossibly high stack of firewood is tied across the animal's back.

"Ernest!" Mallory calls out, her demeanor completely changing.

Ernest swings a leg over and falls to the ground with surprising grace. Placing his hands on his hips he gives Mallory a curt nod before taking in the rest of the group. "What have we got here?"

"Kids from the campground," Professor Tisdale explains. "They wanted to see our site."

Ernest scratches thoughtfully at his fuzzy chin while studying Sam and the others. Pulling a worn leather cowboy hat from his head, he smacks it once against his thigh before pointing it at the effigy. "You tell 'em what this really is?"

"Now Mr. Tucker, we aren't going to discuss this again," Professor Tisdale says with disdain. "How much do I owe you for the wood?"

"Twenty dollars ought to cover it."

Sam can't help herself. "What do you mean, Mr. Tucker?"

Ally jabs her ribs for the second time that day. Sam rubs at them while ignoring Ally's objection and looks expectantly at Ernest Tucker.

The old woodsman slowly replaces his hat and then stares solemnly at Sam with piercing, grey eyes. "It's a warning."

7

A WARNING

"What kind of warning?" Cassy gasps while moving up to Sam's other side.

Ernest Tucker turns and gives a tug at the rope securing the wood. As it clatters to the ground, he gestures to the effigy. "This ancient burial site is protected by the Banshee."

"Mr. Tucker, these kids don't need to be subjected to an old legend," Professor Tisdale says while bending to help collect the wood.

Joseph abandons his pile of dirt to join the group. "Oh, come on, Professor. It's a great story."

"Yeah," Candace adds. The young woman grins mischievously. Her short blonde hair is covered up with a college ballcap to keep the sun out of her eyes, but it sticks out in random tufts, giving her a rather tomboyish appearance. "Didn't you tell us to always investigate everything about the region of a dig? *Including* any local stories or legends, because there's always some small element of truth in there somewhere."

"And the student becomes the teacher," Professor Tisdale says with a wink. Spreading his arms wide in a submissive gesture, he gives a small bow towards the woodsman. "Please, Mr. Tucker. Continue."

"I'd prefer it if you'd call me Ernest." Adjusting his hat one more time, the older man appears to consider the request. "Most people in these parts can recall the stories. But no one has actually heard it since I was a young boy, and that was over sixty years ago."

"The Banshee?" Hunter asks.

Sam looks at her brother and is amused to see how serious he is. He might give her a hard time about her love for mysteries, but they're more alike than he'll ever admit.

Tucker nods at Hunter. "Yup. The original

settlers in this region first wrote about it. The same ones to discover this here mound. Over time, the pioneers built their towns. The location to this place was lost and the Banshee with it, but the story continued."

"What story?" Ally's voice wavers and she moves in closer to Sam. She hates ghost stories and wishes they could just go back to their campsite and forget all about the effigy and the Banshee. But she knows Sam. If they don't find out all they can now, she won't let it go until they do. Better to get it out of the way as soon as possible.

"It's the animal spirit assigned to protect the souls of those entombed in the burial mound," Ernest says solemnly. "Whenever someone gets close to uncovering them, the Banshee returns. It's said to be part animal, part spirit."

"Now, Ernest," Professor Tisdale interrupts. "I explained the last time we met that it's an effigy. Not a burial mound. We don't even know if there are any human remains in there. In the other effigy mounds discovered in North America from this time period, about eighty percent were used to bury the dead. That means twenty percent of them were—"

"Professor, I have an engineering degree. I think I'm capable of doing the math." Ernest's voice is sharp, but his leathered face fails to hide his amusement. Sam suspects he enjoys sparing with the professor and testing their wits.

"Here," Candace says, breaking up the awkward silence. She's holding a printed image and waves it as she brings it over to the group. "This was taken by the drone a few days ago, after we finished clearing the effigy as much as we dared."

Sam crowds around the picture with her friends and is amazed to see what looks like the raised outline of a cat-like animal. The same sort of line drawing you might expect to see inside an ancient cave, except that it's made out of the earth itself on top of the mound. Looking up from the picture, Sam stares at the effigy and can see what must be the head of the animal, closest to them. From this angle it simply appears to be a long series of bumps, like mole holes that have grown over with grass.

"I've seen something like this before," John states. Taking the photo, he studies the details up-close. "In history class. Isn't there a really big snake one somewhere?"

Obviously pleased, Professor Tisdale smiles. "Yes! In Ohio. The Great Serpent Mound. Believed to be constructed in 1070. The most common animals are birds, bear, dear, bison, and lynx, among others. While it's mostly agreed that they were chosen for some sort of religious or spiritual significance, there's no proof that they were meant as protectors or warnings."

"It's a lynx."

Again, the professor smiles, this time at Hunter. "Excellent guess. It is in fact our belief that it was meant to be a lynx."

Sam squints at the picture. She doesn't see it. It could have been the outline of any four-legged animal. "How do you know?"

"We don't for sure," the professor says, confirming Sam's suspicions. "It's based on drawings from more recent findings that also had recorded writings referencing the animals. That, along with historical data and other effigies, has given us a sort of "key" if you will, for deciphering them."

"Lynx are bobcats, right?" John asks.

"They're very similar," Joseph says. "Both native to this area. Used to be more of them. Even seventy years ago, when Ernest's legend was still going strong, there were a lot more lynx around. They've been hunted."

Ernest starts going through the motions of checking the saddle on his mule, clearly signaling his departure. "If you've ever heard a large cat scream, you'll understand how the one from this legend got its name."

"What's the rest of the legend, Ernest?" Sam pushes, eager to hear the story before he leaves.

"People have been disappearing in the mountains since the beginning of time," Ernest says, swinging deftly up onto the saddle. "But around here, it especially seems to correspond with stories of an ancient site. Superstitious folk blamed it on disturbing the dead, while others believed it was simply an unknown animal. Whatever the cause, whenever the cry of the Banshee was heard, it wasn't long before someone went missin.'"

The mule lets out a loud bray, causing Sam to jump and laugh at herself. Even if the story involves a real bobcat, she knows enough about them to realize they aren't normally a dangerous animal. Of course, according to Ernest, the Banshee wasn't normal. Her smile falters.

"The last attack was when I was around ten," Ernest continues. "There was a write-up in the local paper about it. Happened soon after the Sanctuary campground was established if I recall correctly. A man claimed to have found something in the woods, but before he could lead anyone else to his discovery, they were scared off by a strange animal. The man disappeared shortly after." Tipping his hat, Ernest gives his rapt audience a slow wink. "You take care out here, now."

"Wait!" John hollers, running after the mule. "Do you have any more firewood available? We'd like to buy some."

Ernest gives a small chuckle. "Happy to oblige. What's your campsite number? I'll bring some by later."

Sam notices both Ally and Cassy are pressing in close to her. "You two don't really believe that story, do you?"

Cassy stares back at Sam with wide eyes. "I dunno. We've seen stranger things, haven't we?"

Sam considers her friend's answer. She has a point.

Ally glances around at the thick woods behind them. "I don't care if it's true or not, I just want to be back around the campfire before it starts getting dark."

"How long are you guys camping for?" Candace asks. "We should totally all get together for a bonfire or something. And don't worry, we haven't heard any cats screaming the whole week we've been here."

"That's a great idea, but we can't do it tonight," the professor says before Sam can answer. "We're moving our main camp here and still have a lot of work to do before we're done."

"How about tomorrow?" John suggests, having finished his conversation with Ernest. The woodsman has already disappeared down the trail. "We'll have enough wood to make a big fire, so long as it's allowed. You can all come to our site, there's plenty of room."

"There aren't fire restrictions yet," Joseph says. "So I don't think the ranger would mind. What time?"

Sam notices that while Joseph and Candace

are very friendly, Mallory and Isaac look less than thrilled. The other student, Greg, has remained hunched over the work table the whole time they've been there.

"We'll make sure it's going good before dark," Hunters says, clearly excited for any excuse to cook smores.

As they say their goodbyes, Sam tries again to smile at Mallory and this time is rewarded with a small grin. Progress.

"Here kitty, kitty," Hunter taunts from behind Sam, as soon as their group is around the first bend in the trail.

"Hunter…," John warns.

"It's okay," Sam says quickly. Looking back at her brother, she's happy to see the confusion on his face. "Everyone knows it's always the last person in line to get grabbed first."

Hunter glances at the empty trail behind him, and then back at his sister. His eyes narrow.

"Here kitty, kitty," Sam calls mockingly. Yelping, she runs up the trail past Cassy before Hunter can catch her.

8

DR. BURNS

Sam wakes up Sunday morning to the sound of Rocky licking his paw.

"What's wrong with him?" Hunter shoves the rest of his strawberry Pop Tart in his mouth.

"I've spent the past hour trying to figure that out," Sam answers. "I thought something was stuck in his pad, but I can't see anything."

"Poor thing," Ally coos. Taking the poodles face in her hands, she plants a kiss on his warm, black nose. Rocky tolerates the affection but doesn't show his usual enthusiasm for the attention.

"What should we do?" Cassy asks, worried. "We're supposed to go to the lake this afternoon." Hunter gives her a disapproving look. "What? You know what I mean! If he needs a vet, we should figure out what to do soon."

"Who needs a vet?"

Sam turns to see Ranger Nathan Sparks leaning in through the open door of the motor home. His hat is tipped back so that his shiny black hair frames his face, giving him a bit of a dangerous look.

"Um, my dog has something wrong with his paw," Sam explains, her voice strained. Rocky means the world to her. But they're basically in the middle of nowhere and she doesn't have a clue as to what they should do. Lisa left for the office a few minutes ago to see if they had any antibiotic ointment that might work for a dog. She obviously didn't see Nathan.

Nathan's features cloud and he doesn't hesitate. Leaping up the two short steps, he leans down to look at the dog's foot. Rocky licks at his hand. "I don't think it's anything serious," he says after a quick inspection. "But there's probably something in there that needs to come out or else it'll get infected."

"Do you know how to do it?" John asks.

He's sitting next to Hunter at the table, finishing his own easy breakfast.

Nathan shakes his head. "Nope, but a good friend of mine is a veterinarian in Sanctuary."

"She's open on a Sunday?" Ally asks.

Nathan gives her a crooked grin. "No, but she's always available. I can give her call and she'll meet us there. I was heading into town anyway to run some errands so I can give you a lift."

"Give them a lift to where?" Lisa appears next to Nathan, a small tube of Neosporin in one hand. "This was all they had at the camp store."

"Into town," Nathan explains, turning to Lisa. "I was just telling them I know the local vet. I'm sure she can fix Rocky up. I'm afraid he may need more intervention than that," he adds, pointing at the cream.

Lisa nods in agreement. "Are you sure? We don't want to impose."

Nathan's teeth flash white as he smiles warmly. "I'm sure. My truck can seat two other people but I need to leave now for an appointment."

Lisa's brows draw together in a troubled

expression when Ally jumps to Sam's side. "Ally, I don't know how I feel about you two girls alone in town. Maybe I should go, or John."

Hunter drops his head dramatically on the table at the suggestion that his best friend might be taken for the morning. "We were going to go swimming," he whines, looking up from the crook of his arm.

"I promise to keep tabs on them" Nathan interjects. "They'll be welcome at the clinic until I get done with my errands. Sanctuary is normally a very safe place."

"Normally?" Cassy asks, with a hint of humor. "You don't know Sam very well."

Nathan tips his head in Sam's direction. "I have a feeling you and Dr. Burns will get along very well."

Sam grabs Rocky's leash from the coat rack and clips it to his collar before picking him up. She still hasn't figured out why his breed is called a miniature poodle. He's around twenty-five pounds and anything but small.

Ally looks hopefully to Lisa, still standing outside the door. "Please, Lisa? We promise to be on our best behavior. Right, Sam?"

Sam picks her way carefully down the steps and stops in front of Lisa. "Right! Thanks for getting the ointment. Oh!" The purchase makes her think of how expensive an on-call visit to the vet will be. She turns to Nathan. "How am I going to pay Dr. Burns? Can I call my parents from the clinic, maybe?"

"Don't worry about that," Nathan replies as he leads the way to his tan, government-issued truck. "I have a running account there. We can figure it out later."

The half-hour drive into Sanctuary is spent mostly in silence. Sam gets the impression that Nathan Sparks is a man of few words, but when he does speak it's worth listening. As they round what appears to be the last curve of the wooded road and the valley of Sanctuary opens up before them, Sam breaks the silence. "What do you know about the Banshee, Mr. Sparks?"

Nathan peers sideways at her. "Where did you hear about that?"

"From an older man named Ernest when we were visiting the dig site last night," Sam explains.

Nathan chuckles dryly. "Ernest Tucker can weave a tale about pretty much anything and make it sound interesting."

"So, there's not really a Banshee?" Ally asks hopefully.

"That depends on who you're talking to," Nathan says. "There's been some stories circulating about various creatures for as long as there's been settlers in the valley, but no real proof."

"It's supposed to be a lynx," Sam pushes. She's always been curious about legends and this has the potential to be an interesting one.

"Lynx, mountain lion, Big Foot," Nathan laughs louder. "Like I said, it depends on who's doing the telling. Personally, I think they're all likely cases of people who aren't familiar with the region hearing something they don't understand. Whatever it is, I wouldn't worry about it. Hasn't been a "sighting" of anything mysterious that I've heard about for a very long time. The clinic is right up here, on main street."

Sam wishes they had more time to talk about it, but is even more eager to get Rocky taken care of. Nathan had her send a text message once they were close enough for his phone to work, and Sam is relieved to see an old pickup truck parked outside the clinic when they pull up in front.

Climbing out onto the sidewalk, Sam looks up at an old-style wooden sign that reads:

Sanctuary Animal Clinic

The building itself is a historic, single story brick building with a western clapboard storefront to match the rest of main street. It sits on the corner of an intersection, and peering over Rocky's red curls, Sam notes Natures Brew is directly to its left.

Plenty of feet are clapping against the wooden sidewalk around them as tourists and townspeople bustle about. It's not surprising to Sam that it's so busy on a Sunday. It's early July and their annual rodeo is in full swing. Lisa told them all about it when she added it to their agenda. People come from all over the country to participate and watch it.

The shade on the large glass window in front of them snaps up, revealing a tall woman with long, flaming-red hair inside. She smiles warmly at them and gives Nathan a small wave before moving to unlock the door.

"This must be Rocky." The woman wastes no time in assessing her patient, taking him from

Sam even before they cross the threshold.

Ally winks at Sam as they follow the veterinarian inside, approving of the woman's enthusiasm. Although she isn't what Ally expected, there's something about meeting other girls with red hair that creates an immediate bond. She looks to be in her late twenties and is quite attractive but not in a typical way. She has green eyes, like Sam, and unlike most redheads, her skin is a warm bronze. Ally already likes her.

"Sam Wolf, Ally Parker, this is Dr. Ember Burns," Nathan says formally, closing the door behind them.

Dr. Burns pauses and turns back to face them. "Oh, I'm sorry!" she laughs. "I don't mean to be rude. I get a bit single-minded when I have a patient. It's nice to meet you." Easily transferring Rocky into the crook of her left arm, she reaches out her right to shake their hands.

Sam steps forward first and is encouraged by the firm grip. There's a lot to be said about a handshake. "Thank you so much for seeing us, Dr. Burns. I don't know what else I would have done."

Shifting to take Ally's hand, Ember then

waves off the notion. "It's no problem! Really. You saved me from doing some yardwork and it's way too hot out for that. And since it's Sunday you can drop the formality and call me Ember."

Sam returns the other woman's genuine smile before following her down the only hallway. She has an energy that's contagious and like Ally, can't help but instantly like her. Mulling over her first name, it dawns on Sam that Ember must have put up with a lot of teasing in school. She knows how cruel some kids can be with Ally about her red hair, but Ember Burns? Oh, all the options for nicknames…

"Here," Ember is saying while directing them into an exam room. "We'll take a look at what we're dealing with."

"While you've got this under control, I'm going to go run my errands if that's okay?" Nathan asks. "I can be back in about an hour or less."

"That's fine!" Ember answers. "I think us girls will manage."

As the bell over the front door jingles, announcing Nathan's departure, there's the unmistakable sound of clacking nails coming down the hallway. Sam peers curiously out the exam-room door, and then steps back when a huge, cinnamon colored labradoodle bounds inside.

"Oh!" Ally gasps when the friendly dog chooses her first for introductions. Sitting at Ally's feet, she looks up expectantly. Reaching out hesitantly at first, Ally then kneels down to eye-level with the dog when she reacts favorably to the petting.

"That's Daenerys," Ember explains, looking up from Rocky's paw. "Totally harmless and utterly shameless. She will give you a bath in kisses, if you let her."

Laughing now, Ally is working hard to fend off the promised wet tongue of Daenerys. Sam quickly moves in next to her friend, never missing a chance to share some doggy affection.

"I'm impressed," Ember says with obvious respect. "You two last longer than most."

Squealing, Ally finally falls back onto her bottom and then scoots away from the advancing labradoodle. "Okay!" she gasps. "I give in."

Daenerys reacts immediately and sits back,

tongue lolling, giving Ally room to escape. It's clear that the dog understands boundaries and Sam suspects she wouldn't have even licked them at all if they hadn't been open to it. "Good girl," Sam coos, while still petting Daenerys head.

"You were right, Sam," Ember says. "There's some sort of splinter stuck in Rocky's paw. It's not very big but it's deep. I'll need to numb it first so I can dig it out and then I'll clean it and apply some medication to make sure it doesn't become infected."

"Thank you!" Sam says, standing and moving to pet her own dog. He's totally relaxed under Ember's hand and Sam is relieved to see that he isn't at all stressed out.

"It's going to take at least half an hour," Ember explains. "It's probably best if you don't watch. Is there anything you might be interested in checking out while I work on him?"

Sam doesn't hesitate. "Local legends."

Ally gives her friend a sidelong look.

Sam avoids Ally's critical gaze. "Or any historical information about the effigy they're digging at up near the campground."

Ember raises an eyebrow. "Hmmm. Well, the

best place to dig up anything, no pun intended, is at the shop across the street. *Relics of the Past.* Olivia Barker owns it. She has some of the oldest historical archives for the town, as well as some very interesting antiques. She runs a sort of bookstore, slash library corner, too. If anyone has something on old legends, it would be her."

Sam and Ally quickly give Rocky some reassuring hugs before leaving, promising to be back in half-an-hour.

Stepping out into the bright day, Sam squints against the glare as she searches for the store, *Relics of the Past.* When she spots it, a small shiver of premonition dances across her bare arms. It's the same shop she saw the two quarrelling men coming from.

9

RELICS OF THE PAST

Instead of your typical bell ringing over the entrance, when Sam and Ally push the heavy wooden door inward, a resonating gong echoes around them. Jumping slightly, Ally then laughs at herself before smiling back at Sam.

"Cool," Sam whispers. Why she's whispering, she isn't sure. Maybe it's because of the combination of the grand entrance and décor of the store. Plush red drapes hang along the far wall, behind ornate wooden tables laden with what Sam assumes are the promised relics. Incense burns somewhere nearby, offering an exotic flair to the already unusual atmosphere.

"Hello, girls! How may I be of service?"

The loud but friendly voice belongs to an elderly woman, seated in what can only be described as a throne. Like something ripped from a medieval fairytale, the elaborately carved wooden chair is on an elevated platform. It's complete with dragon heads on the top spires and the back is lined with a plush, purple cushion for comfort. It dwarfs who must be Mrs. Olivia Barker, seated daintily on it.

Sam blinks twice before she's sure of what she's seeing. For a moment, her imagination offered Mrs. Barker a matching gown and tiara. However, the woman is wearing a rather plain sundress, and her long grey hair is braided and then wrapped on the top of her head, much like a crown. Deep wrinkles line her friendly face and her blue eyes sparkle with intelligence.

"Too much?"

When Sam and Ally look at each other in confusion, the shop owner cackles.

"My throne, ladies." Standing, she then carefully steps down from the foot-high pedestal and works her way towards the girls. "I picked it up from an on-line auction. I'm told it was used on the set of a rather astute production. Thought it might add some flair to place."

Sam clears her throat. "I, umm… I think it's pretty amazing."

Laughing at Sam's response, the woman stops in front of them and places her hands on her hips. "I'm Olivia Barker, owner and barterer of Relics of the Past. How can I help you young ladies?"

"We're staying at the Sanctuary campground," Sam explains. "There's an archeology dig going on up there that's really interesting so we're hoping to learn something about the effigy they found and any local legends."

"Dr. Burns told us you might have some old historical books," Ally adds. "You know, about scary local ghost stories and stuff."

Mrs. Barker's brows draw together briefly but the look of annoyance is quickly replaced with a friendly grin. "Well girls, I'm afraid I don't know anything about the effy thing. However," Taking each girl by an arm, she steers them towards a back corner of the store. "You may be in luck with digging up some local legends."

Sam's excitement grows when she sees the

large number of old, leather-bound books in a huge bookcase. A quick survey reveals mostly fiction titles, but when Mrs. Barker points to one section, Sam's heart begins to hammer.

"True Stories of Terror to Keep You Up at Night," Ally reads aloud.

Removing the thick book, Sam turns past the title page, stopping at the introduction. "This book is a compilation of first-hand accounts by the men and woman of Sanctuary. Chose to believe what you wish, but often times fact is stranger than fiction."

"Now that's the truth," Mrs. Barker chuckles. "This should give you some fun reading for around the campfire. Can I also interest you in a real geode or maybe a Indian arrowhead?"

Sam shakes her head at the offer. "No thank you, just the book. Oh!" she gasps. "I hope the book is available for loan? I don't think we could afford to buy it."

"If Dr. Burns can vouch for you, I don't see why not," the shop owner says. "I'll need to get your name and where I can contact you at. Just be sure to get it back to me before you leave."

After filling out a form with the required

information, Sam and Ally spend a few more minutes browsing through the interesting items in the store while Mrs. Barker helps other customers. Sam is impressed with the collection of various artifacts. It's like looking through a museum.

When they emerge back outside a short time later, Nathan's truck is pulling up in front of the clinic. As he steps out of the vehicle, he looks surprised to see them crossing the street. "I thought you were going to stay at the clinic. I promised Lisa to keep track of you."

"Sorry," Sam rushes to apologize. "Ember didn't think we'd want to stay and watch her work on Rocky, so she said we could go across the street to the antique store."

Rubbing at his forehead as if fighting a headache, it's clear Nathan's mood has changed since they parted ways. "That's fine, Sam. Ember-- I mean, Dr. Burns was right. What do you have there?" he asks, pointing at the book Sam is clutching to her chest.

"It's a book about local legends!" she says with some excitement. "I thought there might be something about the Banshee in here. It's like

Professor Tisdale says; there's usually some element of truth to them. Maybe there's even something about the effigy that can be helpful."

Nathan frowns again. "I don't think it's a good idea for you kids to get too involved," he says, looking troubled. "I know I told you about it and all, but I think it's best if you stay away from the site. The professor has a limited amount of time to accomplish a lot of work and it really isn't open to the public."

"Sure, Mr. Sparks," Ally answers right away. "The last thing we want to do is get in the way. We've got a busy week, anyway." Taking Sam's arm, Ally leads her friend toward the clinic entrance before she has a chance to say something quarrelsome.

Looking back at Nathan Sparks, Sam resists the urge to ask why the sudden change in opinion. As much as she likes him, Sam's been around enough mysteries and cover-ups to know when someone isn't being truthful.

The Ranger is hiding something.

10

SUNSHINE AND SECRETS

"What do you mean?" Cassy attempts to wipe some sand off of her towel unsuccessfully. "You think he was lying?"

Sam shakes her head. "No, not lying. But Mr. Sparks was definitely being evasive. It was like his whole attitude changed about the dig. Right, Ally?"

Ally shifts uncomfortably on her own towel. Peering up first at the bright-blue sky and then out at the placid mountain lake, she chooses her words carefully. "You were awfully excited about the book, Sam. It might be that Ranger Sparks was regretting telling us about the site because he knows the Professor won't want a bunch of kids nosing around in it." Ally finally looks at Sam and sees the expression she expects. Annoyance. "Remember the whole no mystery thing?"

Cassy puts a hand on each of her friends' legs and then turns a mock glare towards Ally. "Who are we to deny our friend her natural instinct? If we did, we wouldn't have half the fun. It's in her blood, Ally. Her very D-N-A."

Ally giggles.

"What do we call him, anyway?" Cassy continues, having smoothed over the moment. "Mr. Sparks or Ranger Sparks? I'm so confused."

"Ranger, when he's in uniform," John interjects, plopping down in the sand next to Sam. "Same as with police officers."

Sam mulls this over. It makes sense. She doesn't know how much John overheard, but hopes it wasn't very much. Avoiding his gaze, she instead focuses on her brother who's swimming back to shore with broad strokes.

The lake is beautiful. Nestled in between jutting mountains, it reminds her of another lake she and Ally spent time on just the month before, in Montana. The water is almost as clear, and definitely as cold since it's mostly runoff from melting snow. The sand for the beach is likely trucked in, but aside from that and an ice cream cart, the setting is completely natural. Less than a dozen people dot the swim area even though it's a hot day. Sam thought it would be more crowded, especially since the shuttle that makes two runs daily between the campground and the city of Sanctuary makes a stop there.

"Why are you talking about him?" John asks, jarring Sam from her daydreaming.

Before Sam can come up with an honest but vague response, Cassy replies. "Sam thinks he's hiding something."

Sam glares at her.

"Sam…"

Sam cringes. Somehow, when John uses his special "Sam" tone with her it's worse than when her parents do it. "He was just acting weird when he came back to pick us up."

John sighs audibly and Sam shrinks further into her beach towel. "Explain weird."

"All I did was tell him about the book I found and how it might tell us something about the legend and maybe the effigy." Sam picks up a flat rock and considers skipping it across the water, but then drops it after deciding the odds were good that she'd hit someone. She turns finally to face John. "He seemed stressed out and told us we should stay away from the site. That the professor has limited time to get stuff done. Don't you think that's odd?"

"Huh. That *is* sorta strange."

Sam's mouth drops open.

"He was really encouraging about it yesterday," John continues. "I wonder what changed."

Sam considers telling him about the strange men she saw outside the store the day before, but hesitates. John agreeing to something being weird and getting behind investigating a mystery were two different things. She doesn't want to push her luck.

"Did you find anything in the book?" he asks.

Sam tosses another rock down and then looks wishfully at the ice cream cart before answering. "No, not yet. I didn't have a chance to do much more than skim over the chapter list before we had to leave. I didn't want to bring the book here and risk getting the leather cover wet."

Proving her point, Hunter runs up to the group and stops in the middle of them, dripping with lake water. Shaking his mop of wet hair, he manages to get a decent amount of icy drops on all of them.

Squealing, Ally attempts to hide behind Cassy who spreads her arms wide to expand the shield. Laughing, she refuses to give Hunter the victory. "Is that the best you can do?"

"When are you beach bums going to get in the water?" Hunter taunts. He points at Lisa who's lounging a short distance away. "She didn't bring us all the way out here just to lay in the sun. We can do that anywhere."

Sam's been agreeing with her brother an alarming amount lately. Jumping up, she turns and offers a hand to Ally and Cassy. "My brother has a good point. Come on!"

Rocky leaps up from where he's lying near Lisa's feet, alerted to the tone of Sam's voice. He's already walking better and quickly getting back to his playful self.

As Sam hauls her friends to their feet, John also slowly stands, towering over them all, including Hunter. Brushing the sand off his hands on his swim trunks, he smiles crookedly at Sam. "Well, maybe the book will at least have some good ghost stories for the bonfire tonight."

"You don't think we should cancel?" Ally asks.

"Getting together was their idea," Sam points out. "Anyway, it has nothing to do with the dig site. They're coming to our camp, remember?"

"I'm sure if the professor feels like we're interfering with anything, he'll tell us," John agrees. "He doesn't seem like the sort of guy to mince words."

Relieved, Sam pats at her leg to call Rocky to her. She's been looking forward to their get-together tonight. He responds immediately, tongue lolling and she rushes forward towards the water, avoiding any eye-contact with John. Otherwise, he'd probably see right through her. Sam has a strong feeling there's a mystery there somewhere and suspects someone on the dig is a part of it.

11

TALES BY FIRELIGHT

The fire crackles, sending sparks up into the night, lifted by an updraft of hot air. Sam watches them as they briefly flare against the blackness before winking out. It's the perfect setting for the story Hunter is reading to them from the book of legends.

"What was that? The man cried, turning toward the sounds coming from the nearby woods." Hunter's eyes reflect the firelight, and it's obvious he relishes the dramatic tension. Standing in front of the large group of teens and young adults, he waves his right hand in the air for emphasis while holding the old book with his left.

"I didn't realize he had it in him," Cassy whispers, eliciting a small giggle from Ally.

"We used to put on plays in the family room for mom and dad all the time," Sam says, smiling at the memory. "Hunter always stole the spotlight."

"Suddenly, a growl that was neither man nor beast ripped through the night." Pausing, Hunter looks slowly around at his audience before continuing. "Was it Big Foot or Sasquatch? A hunter or the prey? The townsfolk would never know because Harvey Earlfinker never returned and to this day has not been found."

Slapping the book shut, Hunter hops over a log before sitting down between Sam and Cassy. "Well, there's no doubt *this* story is true!"

"Why do you say that?" Joseph asks, chuckling at the suggestion.

Hunter gives his head a shake and widens his eyes, as if the answer is obvious. "Because no one would ever make up a name like Earlfinker. Gotta be real."

Cassy gives Hunter a small shove before handing him a s'more. "Stop it. You're going to give Ally nightmares."

"I don't think anything could be more terrifying than the grizzly Sam faced," Ally says, eating her own chocolaty morsel.

"Oh, my gosh!" Candace exclaims from across the fire. "What happened?"

"I'm sure whatever it is, it's exaggerated," Mallory snips.

Sam's face reddens. "It wasn't like I "faced" him. He came after me. We were in Alaska," she adds, realizing why Mallory would think the story wasn't true. Although grizzlies were once native to the Cascade Mountains, it was extremely rare to see one this far south nowadays. "Rocky helped distract him until luckily, another grizzly made him leave."

"What story is next?" Ally asks before Mallory has a chance to respond.

"Did you find anything in there about the Banshee?" Candace questions. "Big Foot is great and all, but I'd like to hear some firsthand accounts of this lynx thing if it's something that's supposed to be around here."

"A Banshee?" Lisa pauses while reaching for a marshmallow stick.

"I'm afraid the local gentleman Mallory arranged to have deliver our wood and other supplies is also a bit superstitious," Professor Tisdale explains. "He told the kids about a local legend involving a lynx-like cat called The Banshee. He somehow managed to tie it into the animal image on the effigy. Quite the imagination, really."

Lisa looks skeptically first at Sam, and then at the book. "I'm sure your borrowing this book today had nothing to do with digging further into that connection?"

Sam squirms on the log, trying to avoid eye contact by taking her time to very carefully place a bite of chocolate on a graham cracker. When she finally finishes sandwiching a melted marshmallow, she looks up to discover Lisa still watching her. Sighing, she accepts defeat. "I thought it would be interesting. But it doesn't matter, because I didn't find a story about it. At least, I don't think there's one based on the titles. There is something that sounds even more interesting," she rushes, not giving Lisa a chance to question her motives. "It's one called 'Ancient Mound of Spirits'. I didn't get a chance to read any of it, but I thought it could have something to do with the effigy."

Professor Tisdale doesn't look up from the fire he's poking at but after dropping a log onto it, he makes a small grunting sound. "Perhaps. Although I suspect there are plenty of ghost story themes involving graveyards and such."

Sam licks the remnants of chocolate from her fingers before taking the book from Hunter. Thumbing through it, she attempts to find the story in question. "How in the world were you able to read this?" she says to Hunter while holding it up to the firelight.

"Haven't we had enough stories?" Mallory wipes her hands on her jeans and then turns to look at Isaac. "You brought your guitar, right? I'd rather listen to that."

The suggestion is met by encouraging shouts to Isaac, including Cassy, who claps her hands when he eventually picks up the guitar from the ground behind where he's seated.

Sam shrugs her shoulders and smiles at Ally's questioning look. "She's probably right," she whispers. Looking back down at the book, she discovers it's open to the story she was looking for. Skimming the first few lines, she then nudges Ally and leans in close. "Hey, listen to this: The existence of the mound of sacred bones was a tale told by those who dwelled in this land long before the settlers arrived. Though never found, the lost valley where it sits is said to be marked by the rock of two-feathers, the spirit guide of its creators."

"Shhh," Hunter mutters around yet another s'more.

Making a face at her brother, Sam closes the book. "That doesn't sound like the effigy," she whispers to Ally.

"Not unless the valley disappeared in the past hundred years or so," Ally snickers.

"Still…" She knows there's something of significance that she's missing. Glancing up, she finds Mallory watching her, the shadows caused by the fire dancing across her face.

***

Sam jerks awake with a start. Confused, she wipes at her eyes against the pitch-blackness of the interior of the motorhome. What woke her up?

"Sam?" Cassy whispers. "Are you awake? Did you hear that?"

"I'm awake," Sam croaks. Clearing her throat, she pushes at Ally's sleeping form beside her. "What was it?"

Cassy stumbles toward the bed Sam and Ally are sharing at the back of the trailer. "I don't know. It was like a… screeching."

"What, huh?" Ally mutters. "What's wrong?"

"Probably nothing." Sam sits up straight, a small surge of adrenaline quickly chasing the sleep away. "Maybe an owl?" The barn owls that occupy the woods around their homes can sometimes put on quite a show, sounding like a screaming woman.

A long, not-too-distant shriek erupts again. This time, Sam clearly hears it. "That's not a barn owl."

Rocky growls low in his throat, the kind of warning he reserves for special occasions. Reaching out in the dark, Sam places a comforting hand on his back, but her heart races even faster.

"Girls?" Lisa emerges at the top of the three

steps leading to her room. Reaching around the corner, she fumbles briefly before finding the light switch. It clicks audibly several times, but nothing happens.

Leaping up from the bed, Sam stubs her toe on the leg of the table as she stumbles into the small kitchen space. Pulling open a drawer, she digs around and comes up with a flashlight. Just as she clicks it on, there's a banging at the door.

"Oh!" Gasping, Sam jumps back from the door, dropping the light on the floor.

"Hey!" John calls, knocking again. "Open up!"

Laughing nervously, Lisa reaches the door first and opens it as Sam retrieves the light. "You boys all right out there? That's quite an owl."

"I don't think that's an owl," John replies, echoing Sam's statement.

"It's coming from the woods behind our tent," Hunter explains. "Sounds like a big cat, if you ask me."

"No one asked you," Cassy retorts. "It's an owl."

Another scream drifts through the camp and John slams the door behind them. After a moment of consideration, he also locks it.

12

WATERFALLS AND ROGUES

Monday morning comes a few short hours later, and Sam wakes to Cassy's foot pushing into the small of her back. The three girls are crowded into the pullout bed, while John and Hunter share the small bed in the table space.

They'd sat huddled in the motorhome for over half an hour, waiting for any further sounds that never came. Lisa finally ordered them all to bed, and wouldn't allow the boys to go back outside.

Now, they've slept in. Sam searches out the

one clock but the face is dark. She forgot that the power was out. Frowning, she pushes herself up. Even if the power in the campground is out, the trailer has a battery. She doesn't know much about that stuff, but it seems like it should still be working.

Slipping out from under the tangle of arms and legs that are Ally and Cassy, Sam nearly steps on Rocky. "Sorry!" she whispers, stepping around her furry friend.

"Hey."

Sam looks up to find John sitting in the murky, early morning light filtering in through he shades. "Hey. I'm trying to figure out what time it is. We're supposed to meet the guide near the pool at nine for the hike to the waterfall."

John struggles to shift in the small space, but manages to reach his phone. "It's only eight."

Relieved, Sam reaches for a box of pop tarts. "Why do you think the power is out? Isn't there a battery or something?"

John scratches at his head. "Yeah." Without another word, he slides out from under the thin blanket. Taking one of the pop tarts Sam offers, he opens the door, squinting against the flood of light.

Sam scrambles to follow him outside. It's another gorgeous day. Pausing, she takes a deep breath of crisp air. It always has a special quality to it early in the morning. Sam normally isn't an early riser, but when she's camping, she makes an exception. Energized, she skips around the motorhome and finds John holding the long electrical cord. He has a puzzled look on his face.

"What's wrong?"

Holding the cord out, he gives his head a small shake. "It was unplugged."

"Unplugged?" Sam looks around the camp. Nothing looks disturbed. They'd been up late with the professor and his students, but they all left before midnight. The power was working when they went to bed. Moving toward the campfire, Sam glances at the mix of wood stumps and camp chairs. They'd been careful not to leave any food out and there really wasn't anything else of interest. Sam pauses.

"Well this is weird," John says, his voice a mix of confusion and anger. He's standing at the rear of the motorhome with a side compartment open and his head stuck partway inside. Standing up, he turns to face Sam. "The battery is disconnected. Is someone playing a prank on us? Why would someone do this?"

Sam crosses her arms over her chest, her suspicions confirmed. "It wasn't a prank." When John stares at her silently, she sighs and points to the picnic table near the tent. "That's where I left it last night. The book of legends is gone."

***

"I'm sorry, Sam, it just doesn't make any sense," Cassy says while scrambling over a fallen tree. Reaching the other side, she turns to give Ally a hand. "Why in the world would anyone go to all of the effort of chasing us into a dark motorhome so they can steal an old book?"

"I have to agree," Ally says. Dropping down beside Cassy, she watches as Sam and Rocky scramble across the log. "If someone wanted it, they could have just gone to the store and bought or borrowed it, like we did."

Sam watches as John and Hunter get farther ahead of them on the trail and waits until she's sure they won't overhear her. "Unless they didn't know about it until last night."

Cassy huffs. "So now you think one of the archeology students took it?"

Sam shrugs. "Either that, or someone else who just figured out there's something in that book they don't want anyone else to know."

"I'm not following." Ally loops an arm through Sam's and urges her forward. She doesn't want to get too far behind the group. There's close to a dozen campers on the hike, which promises a spectacular waterfall at the end of the three-mile trail.

"I can't quite put my finger on it yet, Ally," Sam confesses. "I think there's more to this effigy site than we're being told. Something weird is going on in these woods."

"Whoa," Cassy blurts out, moving up to Sam's other side as the trail temporarily widens. "That's quite a leap."

"Which is why I'd rather we keep it to ourselves," Sam whispers, jerking her chin in the boys' direction. "But you have to admit that there's got to be a reason behind what happened last night. Someone really wanted that book and we need to figure out why."

"We do?" Ally asks, looking pointedly at Sam.

"You know it's going to happen whether we agree to it or not," Cassy laughs.

John looks back in response to the laughter, and Sam nudges Cassy before slowing down and forcing the other girls to hang back with her. "I'm not saying we should *do* anything, just… pay attention. And tomorrow, when we take the shuttle into town for the rodeo, we can get online and do some of our own research into these effigy things."

"What do you think we're going to find?" Ally questions.

Sighing, Sam's shoulders sag. "I have no idea."

Removing her arm, Ally then drapes it across Sam's shoulders. "Don't worry. Even if we fail to uncover a real mystery, I'm sure we'll have a blast at the rodeo tomorrow night."

"Yeah!" Cassy agrees. Yelping, she hops over a large root before being forced to scoot ahead due to the trail narrowing again. Stopping, she turns to look back at Sam and Ally to comment on what's sure to be a great show. Instead, she tilts her head questioningly at something beyond them.

Sam and Ally also stop, and Sam stares questioningly at Cassy's silent, puzzled expression. "What is it?" she asks, looking behind them. The trail is empty, but she catches movement from some underbrush off to the side about fifty feet back.

"I just saw two guys back there," Cassy says slowly. Her eyes flicker in Sam's direction. "Two rough looking guys in their twenties, dressed like cowboys and carrying very large backpacks. They disappeared into the trees."

Sam's eyes widen and she quickly scoots back the way they just came.

"Sam, wait!" Ally whispers, hurrying after her.

Estimating where Cassy saw tree branches moving, Sam slows down and studies the terrain.

"There," Cassy states, pointing a few feet farther back.

Sure enough, there's a smaller, barely perceivable trail branching off from the main one.

"Ally!" John's voice echoes down the trail.

Making up her mind, Sam doesn't waste any time. She takes several quick steps into the foliage just in time to see the backs of the two men disappear down a steep dip in the trail. But it was enough.

"Sam!" Cassy is right behind her. "We have to go back. We're going to get lost and Lisa will never let us go on another trip by ourselves again."

"Okay." Sam breathes, trying to control her racing heart. Moving swiftly back to where Ally is still waiting, she reaches her just as John and Hunter come back into view. "We're coming, guys!" she calls out, waving her hand.

Cassy silently rejoins them and the three girls move toward the waiting brothers. But Sam is grinning.

"What is it?" Ally asks cautiously. "I've seen that look before."

Sam's smile widens. "It was the same two guys from the store," she says. "And I think I know what they're doing."

"How could you possibly know that?" Cassy gasps.

Stopping, Sam turns in the same direction the

other trail was leading and points up at a nearby mountain peak, jutting above the tree line. At its precipice is a unique rock formation in the shape of two feathers rising starkly against the blue sky.

Sam's green eyes sparkle with excitement. "The lost valley."

13

HUNTER OR HUNTED

"My legs were already killing me. I can't believe I let you talk me into going on *another* hike!" Cassy pauses to take a drink from her water bottle while looking pointedly at Sam.

"I'm okay with the extra exercise," Ally says, "but I don't think it's a good idea to go on an unmarked trail."

Sam does her best not to sigh too loudly. She's thankful her friends are here, even though they don't really believe her about the lost valley. Unfortunately, while Sam distinctly recalls the legend stating the way to the lost valley was marked by rocks in the shape of two feathers, Ally and Cassy weren't really listening when she read it the night before. With the book now missing, it's impossible to prove it. However, the fact that the book *itself* is missing makes it all the more suspicious. Especially since they saw those two guys in the woods earlier.

Sam gazes up the trail past Cassy, doing her best to estimate how far they've come. It was three miles to the waterfall, which turned out to be just as gorgeous as promised, and she thinks the deer trail isn't more than a half-mile in. They should be getting close. At least, she hopes they are, because it'll be dinner time soon. It won't get dark for a few more hours, but the shadows always thicken early in the woods. "We won't go far. I promise," she says to Ally. "Just enough to see where it leads, or if the deer trail connects with a bigger one. A quick peek and then we'll go right back."

"And if we find anything?" Cassy asks, putting her water bottle back in her pack.

Sam kicks at a loose rock near her foot. "We'll tell Lisa. Or Ranger Sparks."

"Why don't we just tell them now?" Ally

suggests. "Or wait for the boys to finish swimming so they can go with us."

Sam pushes her bangs back off her forehead. It's still rather hot out. "Because we don't really have anything to tell them, and the boys will just make fun of us." When Ally doesn't respond, Sam presses further. "If I go to the park ranger with a wild theory based on something I read out of an old book that we don't even have anymore, and a legend that he doesn't even think is true, about a possible lost valley that a couple of creepy guys from town are trying to find, what do you think he's going to say?"

Ally blinks.

"She has a point," Cassy says.

The three girls stare silently at each other for a few heartbeats. Ally is the first to giggle, quickly followed by Cassy, and then Sam.

Sam is the first to recover. Wiping the tears from her eyes, she kneels down next to Rocky to reassure him that they haven't gone crazy. He whimpers slightly as she hugs him. "Seriously, guys, you know me. I'm sure it's nothing. Just a bunch of random stuff that may or may not go together. I just want to make sure."

“Yeah, we do know you,” Ally replies, serious again. “That’s just it. You see things that others don’t, Sam.”

“She’s right,” Cassy agrees. “So, I guess this means we’re going to find us a deer trail, and maybe a lost valley? Cuz actually, the lost valley part sounds pretty cool.”

“I think it might be around the next bend.” Sam stands and rubs her hands together. “I dropped a branch across the trail behind me on our way out when I spotted it, to make finding it easier later on.”

Smart, Cassy mouths, walking again. Encouraged, Sam falls in behind her with Ally. “Maybe we’ll get back in time to go swimming before dinner.”

“I hope so,” Ally replies. “Either that, or I need a shower. I think I’ve got about half an inch of trail dirt stuck to me!”

Before Sam can agree, a distinct rustling sound reaches them from nearby. Something, or someone is moving around in the woods. Cassy freezes, obviously hearing it, too.

"What was that?" Ally whispers, her eyes wide.

Although a popular hike with the campers in the park, this late in the day, they haven't encountered anyone out on the trail. It's also a Monday, meaning traffic in the campground is already at a minimum. The solitude makes them feel even more vulnerable.

"Probably a deer," Sam suggests.

Rocky growls, the hairs at the base of his neck rising.

Cassy slowly walks backwards until she's huddled with Ally and Sam. A large branch snaps, pinpointing the movement to about fifty feet away and off to their left. The ground slopes here, and when combined with the gathering shadows in the thick pine trees, it makes it impossible to see what's there.

"Maybe we should go back," Sam mutters. "We can go exploring later with John and Hunter. I don't care if they think I'm silly."

But as they turn to leave, a shriek identical to the one they heard the night before erupts from the woods, even closer than the snapping branch. Rocky's barking blends in with the noise, adding to the confusion as the girls stagger backwards.

"Come on!" Sam yells, pulling at Rocky's

leash. He refuses to move. For a frantic moment, she watches as Ally and Cassy move away down the trail as another wail washes over her. "Come *on*, Rocky!"

Finally, the poodle gives in and reluctantly follows Sam. Stumbling over a rock, Sam catches her balance and awkwardly runs while limping and pulling on the leash at the same time. She can't tell if there's the sound of pursuit behind her and she's too scared to stop and find out.

Coming around a curve, she looks up to see how far away her friends are, but instead gasps as she nearly runs into them. They've been forced to stop because taking up the width of the trail is Ernest Tucker, and he doesn't look happy.

***

"What are you gals doing out here so late?" Ernest Tucker growls, his white bushy eyebrows drawn together in consternation.

Sam fights against her initial reaction to throw the same question back at the older man. But she's learned to have a healthy respect for her elders, especially a rugged mountain man.

It's hard to tell exactly how old Mr. Tucker is. Sam figures somewhere between sixty and eighty. He doesn't have his mule with him – or any wood. All he has is a long, crooked walking stick which is worn smooth around the top from years of use.

Sam clears her throat, which has gone uncomfortably dry.

"We… we're just out for a walk," Ally says her voice wavering.

Mr. Tucker turns his focus to Ally and perhaps realizing he gave them a fright, takes a step backward and relaxes his stance. "I apologize if I startled you but I heard some screaming. When I saw you running, I figured you might have fallen into some trouble. Was that you I heard?"

"No!" Cassy blurts. "It was the—"

"It was probably an owl," Sam interrupts. Trying her best to laugh it off she ignores the reactions from Cassy and Ally. "We heard something in the trees. Then, the screeching started and, well… after hearing your story, Mr. Tucker, I think our imaginations got away with us."

The old mountain man stares at Sam for so long that the silence becomes deafening in the wake of the screams. "I told y'all to call me Ernest," he finally says, wiping at his nose. "It's best you be going back, now. These woods are no place for you to be in the dark."

Pulling at Rocky's leash, Sam is the first to move past him, but she pauses after only a few steps. "Ernest, I could be wrong. About the owl, I mean. Be careful."

Laughing heartily, Ernest gives his worn flannel shirt a tug. "I appreciate the concern, Sam, but I've managed okay in these mountains for more than seventy years."

Well. That answers the question about his age.

The three girls wave their goodbyes and head back toward the campground, with Ernest still chuckling.

"Why didn't you tell him we thought it was the Banshee?" Cassy asks once they're a decent distance away. "Of all the people we could tell, I think he's the most likely to believe us."

"That's exactly why I didn't," Sam replies.

Cassy and Ally both stop. Looking back at

Sam they're clearly perplexed. "What do you mean?" Ally asks.

The corner of Sam's mouth rising slightly, she places both of her hands on her hips. "If Ernest had really heard the Banshee before like he said, then he should have been able to tell *us* that was the Banshee screaming." Sam watches as the realization settles over her friends faces. "I don't think there really *is* a Banshee. There never was!"

14

CURIOUSER AND CURIOUSER

"His foot is healing up nicely." Dr. Ember Burns releases Rocky's paw before giving him a pat on the head. "I don't think you have anything to worry about, Sam. He can go back to all of his regular activities. Just be sure to clean it off at the end of the day."

Sam breathes a sigh of relief. She figured Rocky was fine, but hearing it from Ember makes her feel much better. Cassy and Ally are gathered behind her in the lobby of the Sanctuary Animal Clinic. For late-morning on a Tuesday she's surprised at how busy the town is. Of course, a good percentage of them are likely tourists going to the rodeo that afternoon, same as them.

"Are you going to the rodeo?" Ember asks.

Sam smiles at how predictable they are. "Yes! We rode the shuttle over."

"My sister and their brothers are out doing the tourist thing before we meet up later," Cassy explains. "I'm thinking we need to go stop in at Nature's Brew again."

Ember nods in agreement. "My vet assistant, Mel, is working an extra shift over there today. She's normally here during the week, but with the rodeo in full swing, they need the help more than I do."

"We met Mel!" Ally smiles broadly.

"Yes, well, she's memorable," Ember laughs. "And a great friend. Tell her you're clients of mine and you'll get a ten percent discount."

"It's settled, then," Cassy announces.

Sam isn't so eager to spend more of her money on a sugary drink, but then raises an eyebrow as an idea forms. "Do they have Wi-Fi?"

"Yes, they do," Ember confirms. "I know you don't have anything out at the campground.

Most kids would be going crazy by now."

Sam simply nods in agreement, but she catches a look from Ally. Her best friend knows that Sam couldn't care less about social media. It's information she's after.

"I was wondering if I could ask you one more thing." Sam kneels down to pet both Rocky and the young vet's dog, Daenerys, at the same time. They look like they could be relatives, with Rocky being the smaller version of the labradoodle.

Ember tips her head questioningly at Sam. "Sure! Fire away."

"Have you ever heard an old story about a Banshee? It's supposed to be some sort of large cat, like a lynx," Sam explains.

Ember scrunches up her nose before shaking her head. "Nope. I grew up in Sanctuary, and I'm familiar with pretty much all of the popular scary stories and legends. I don't remember hearing of anything like that. Why do you ask?"

Sam briefly explains the story Ernest told them, and the following "encounters." She makes sure to emphasize how they think it's an owl, so their new friend doesn't think them too gullible.

"What does the animal sound like?" Ember asks in all seriousness.

Before Sam can reply, the front door dings, announcing the arrival of Ranger Sparks. He's in uniform, and he removes his hat when he sees them. "Hey, Ember. You free for lunch soon?"

Blushing slightly, Ember waves him over. "Sure, Nathan. I'm just finishing up with Rocky. We're talking about Ernest and some Banshee tale he told the girls. Anyone at the campground report any weird sounds the past couple days?"

Sam cringes. Discussing this with the ranger is the last thing she wants to do after his reaction to the book she borrowed. At the thought of the book, Sam winces again. She isn't looking forward to the visit they have to make to let Mrs. Barker know the book is missing. Between the vet visit and what is sure to be a pricey book, her parents aren't going to be very happy about the extra expenses for the trip.

"Actually," Nathan answers without any sign of irritation, "I did have a couple of campers mention it. One of 'em is very familiar with the area and swears it isn't an owl."

"You said you have brothers?" Ember directs

the question at Sam who nods in confirmation. "And were they there for Ernest's story?" Sam nods again. "Well, I think the most likely answer then is that someone's playing a prank on you."

Ally starts to protest, but Sam puts a hand out to stop her. Of course, John would never go along with something like that but if it frees them up to keep investigating it, it didn't hurt to let Ember and Nathan believe it.

"Even if it's a bobcat or lynx, they're both relatively harmless and rarely ever attack people," Ember adds. "They're not normally very vocal, but when they are it can sound like a baby crying or woman screaming. Just be aware of your surroundings, and where your brothers are, and you should be fine."

"I don't like letting Ranger Sparks think John would do something like that," Ally complains a few minutes later as they cross the street to Nature's Brew.

"We didn't say he would," Cassy replies. Pulling the door to the coffee shop open, she turns to look back at Sam and Ally. "But you know Lisa. Even if Ranger Sparks tells her bobcats aren't anything to worry about, she'll probably ban us from all of the trails. I say we continue to keep the whole encounter to ourselves and let everyone else think the other night was a prank."

Sam walks through the door slowly, feeling guilty. While Lisa is Cassy's older sister, she's her and Ally's teacher so their relationship is different.

"How about we enjoy being tourists the rest of the time we're here, and promise to report it right away if we hear it again?" Ally suggests.

Sam is already on her phone, connecting to the internet. Her finger hovers over the search key and she looks up at Ally. "Sure, but that doesn't mean we can't umm… look into *other* things, does it?"

Laughing, Ally drags Sam over to one of the few small tables and directs her to sit in one of the chairs. "You mean like lost valleys and rocks that look like feathers?"

Sam wrinkles her nose at Ally before laughing with her. "Exactly."

"Search away," Cassy says waving her hands. "Me? I think there's a double-tall mocha mint latte calling to me."

"It'll stunt your growth," Ally says, jumping up to follow her to the back of a line. "I think I'll get another Italian soda. Coming?"

Sam shakes her head at Ally's question and begins reading the search results. By the time the other two girls return and plop down on either side of her, Sam is overflowing with excitement.

"Uh-oh," Ally says.

Cassy looks at Sam in alarm. "What? Oh. You're right, Ally. We're about to wish this place didn't have Wi-Fi."

Ignoring her friends teasing, Sam jumps right into what she found. "No hits for anything about a Banshee or bobcat story in Sanctuary. I didn't find any articles or news stories about the dig at the campground, either, but I suppose that isn't something they'd go to the press with until after it was done."

"So, what then?" Ally presses. "You look like the Cheshire cat!"

"Mound builders," Sam states. When Cassy and Ally give her blank stares, she grins and continues. "That's the name given to the people who built the effigies, but they also built platform mounds or flat-topped pyramids."

"Pyramids?" Ally asks her interest growing.

Sam nods eagerly. "Yup. There's been a bunch of them found in the states, but not this far west. I guess the largest one in America is as big as the Egyptian Giza pyramid."

"What? Why haven't we ever heard about these?" Cassy asks.

Sam shrugs. "Maybe we will when we get into more historical stuff in school. They're not made the same way as Egyptian pyramids. They're mostly mud and stuff, with a flat top where wooden buildings used to be. But, the most interesting part, is that the effigy mounds are often found near them. Like, they're markers or maybe part of an old settlement with the flat-top mound in the middle."

"The lost valley," Cassy whispers, leaning in. "You think it might actually be out there?"

"What would anyone want with it?"

Ally's question is very reasonable, and Sam turns to her with a determined look on her face. "Because finding one here would be like hitting the jackpot for someone who knows what it is. The effigy is a small example of what sort of relics could be in a mound pyramid. I think the lost valley is there, and whoever is stealing from it is trying to scare us away."

"What are we going to do?" Cassy asks. "We don't have any proof."

Ally and Sam look at each other, and when Ally doesn't object, Sam swallows hard and sets her mouth in grim line. "Then we find some."

15

WATCH YERSELF, PARTNER

"That wasn't nearly as bad as we thought it would be." Cassy stops a short distance down the boardwalk from Relics of the Past. Holding a hand above her eyes, she attempts to look down the street. "I'm ready for lunch. Let's find someplace to eat before we have to get Rocky and meet everyone at the rodeo."

Sam sometimes envies her friends ability to move on from one issue to the next without any pause. She'd been so stressed out over how Mrs. Barker was going to react, she hadn't even thought about lunch. Fortunately, not only did

Mrs. Barker not charge them a huge amount for the lost book, she laughed it off and refused to accept any payment. Apparently, they were the first customers to even look at the book in over two years. Sam insisted they all buy a souvenir so she now has a small bag containing three Indian arrowheads. She's going to give one to Ember as a thank you for being so nice about Rocky and offering to keep him at the clinic with her while they explored the town.

"Ember mentioned a restaurant yesterday," Sam says thoughtfully. "But I can't remember what it's called."

"The Rusty Wagon Wheel," Ally says with a grin. "Down that a way, partners."

Sam looks to the far end of the block they're standing on and can see what looks like an old, wooden wagon wheel leaning up against a light post. She's about to make a joke when she sees two familiar forms exit the building and head in their direction.

With a small gasp, Sam reaches out to grab at Cassy and Ally. Without any explanation, she drags them back past the antique shop and then one store beyond, until they're standing behind a huge chainsaw carving of a bear. The carving competition is a favorite highlight of the rodeo events and the town is littered with various statues.

Used to her friend's unusual behavior, Ally complies without protest and simply raises her eyebrows at her once they've stopped.

Cassy isn't so easily manhandled. Shaking Sam's hand off her arm, she turns to her with an exasperated look. "Sam! Is there a game of hide-and-seek going on that I don't know about?"

"Our friends are back," Sam states. Leaning slowly to her left she peeks out from behind the bear. "And they're coming this way."

Tilting her head quizzically, Cassy goes along with the ploy and squats down so that her eyes line up with the bear's outreached arm opposite Sam. "It's the guys from the woods!"

"The same two I saw the first day we were in town," Sam confirms. Watching them as they work their way through the crowded boardwalk, she notes they're wearing the same clothes as before, except now they're quite dirty. The larger of the two has a duffle bag draped over his shoulder. Just before the men reach the entrance to Relics of the Past, another man suddenly appears from in between the buildings, intercepting them.

"It's Ernest!" Cassy whispers.

"What?" Ally presses up against Sam's back, cautiously getting in on the spying.

Sam holds her breath as the three men begin to have an animated conversation. The taller of the three points a finger at Ernest and after a moment, jabs him roughly in the chest. In a motion defying his age, Ernest grabs ahold of the younger man's forearm and twists it violently, bringing him down on one knee. The ruffian recovers quickly, however, and lurches to his feet, shoving Ernest back at the same time, breaking his hold.

Sam begins to step out from behind their hiding spot. How she's going to help, she doesn't know, but she can't just watch while they hurt Ernest. Ally puts a restraining hand on Sam's arm, and she's about to shake it off when she sees the scuffle is already over. A few passersby noticed the altercation and slowed to watch, causing the two younger men to move away. Ernest, hands on his hips, glares at them as they enter the antique shop.

"What in the world was that about?" Ally whispers, her hand still tightly clutching Sam.

Sam ducks back behind the carved bear when Ernest starts to look around to take stock of who's watching. After a moment, she dares to peek out again and sees his retreating form about halfway down the block. "Come on," she urges, tugging Ally's arm to encourage her.

The three girls scurry past the antique store without looking inside. With lunchtime approaching, the tourists are coming out in full force, and the girls soon get lost in the crowd.

"Where'd he go?" Cassy says after they've walked nearly all the way to the restaurant. "I lost him."

"I don't know why we're trying to follow him," Ally huffs, dodging a small child with a dripping ice cream cone.

"We're not really following him," Sam counters. "He just happens to be going in the same direction as we are."

"Good!" Cassy exclaims as they stop next to the wagon wheel. "Then we can go in and eat. I'm starving!"

As Sam turns to lead the way inside, she catches a glimpse of Ernest Tucker's conspicuous mass of white hair nearby. Turning back toward him, a young couple holding hands move past her, creating a gap in the crowd and a clear view of who he's talking to. Spinning away from Tucker, her face a mask of fury, is Mallory.

16

DANGEROUS LIAISON

"Now I understand what all the hype is about." John walks in a wide circle around the intricate, wooden chainsaw carving of an eagle. It's also been painted, highlighting a salmon clutched in its talons in mid-flight.

Sam nods in agreement. The afternoon has been full of a carnival-like atmosphere complete with rides, street-fair, multiple competitions for viewing, and of course, the rodeo.

After ducking inside the Rusty Wagon Wheel, they had an amazing lunch before meeting up with the rest of the gang. Lisa has taken Rocky with her on the shuttle, back to the camp. She's had her fill of fun already, and the girls can't take Rocky into the stadium to watch the rodeo. The rest of them plan on catching the next ride back to the campground in a couple of hours.

Sam and Ally exchange a look. Ally wants to tell her brother about what they witnessed, but Sam isn't so sure it's a good idea.

"Corn dogs!" Hunter shouts.

Cassy, easily forgetting about the debate when distracted by the idea of more food, loops an arm through Hunter's. "Lead the way. I'll buy the first round."

"Cassy!" Ally shouts at their retreating backs.

Cassy looks over her shoulder and gives her friend a wink. "We'll meet you at the entrance to the stadium in half-an-hour, before the barrel racing starts!"

Shaking his head, John rubs his stomach. "It makes me nauseous just watching your brother eat all day, Sam. I don't know how he does it."

Laughing, Sam looks again at Ally. Even though she knows John will accurately accuse her of being a busy-body, she also knows that Ally is right. They might not have enough information to figure out how it all ties together, but their brothers have proven helpful in the past and always come through for them.

"John, we think something weird is going on with Ernest, Mallory, and a couple of guys we've seen a few times."

John stops rubbing his stomach and stares at Sam. "Two scruffy-looking dudes in bad flannel trying too hard to fit in?"

Trying and failing to hide her surprise, Sam takes a step closer to him and lowers her voice. "Yes. Where have *you* seen them?"

"Yesterday, when you guys were out on your walk, Hunter and I decided to go visit the dig site. We ran into them on the trail on our way there." John scratches at his head and gazes first at Sam and then Ally. "We tried to say hi and introduce ourselves, but they literally shoved past us."

"I knew it!" Sam mutters.

"Knew what?" John presses.

Sam crosses her arms over chest and lets out a puff of air, deciding to share everything. It only takes a few minutes to bring him up-to-date, including her theory about the lost valley and what she found during her internet search. "Then, right before lunch, we saw Ernest get in an argument with those two before meeting with Mallory," she finishes. "And Mallory looked very angry."

"She always looks mad," Ally points out, causing Sam to laugh.

"You mean like now?" John asks while nodding to a point behind them.

Turning around, Sam spots the girl in question. Sure enough, Mallory isn't standing more than twenty feet away, glaring at them. When she sees she has their attention, she raises a hand and makes a motion for them to follow her before spinning around and walking quickly away.

Before giving it any thought, Sam follows.

"Sam, wait!" John calls out.

Not wanting to lose sight of Mallory in the crowd, Sam slows slightly but doesn't look behind her. The rodeo grounds are massive, taking up several acres at the far end of town. It's broken up into different sections and they're now moving into the farthest corner, where a series of corrals leads away from the stadium. The wooden fencing is interspersed with trailers and small sheds, used for unloading and moving various animals.

John reaches Sam's side as they round the corner of yet another small building, revealing more fencing of a lesser-used area. The echoing voice of an announcer reaches them, stating the next event begins in fifteen minutes.

Stopping partway up the next corral, Sam scrunches up her nose. "I lost her."

"Well, if she wants to talk to us, why lead us on a wild goose chase?" Ally says with some irritation, stopping in between her brother and Sam.

"Good question," Sam mutters, kicking at a clump of dirt. Wiping at the sweat beading at the base of her neck, she's suddenly eager to get into the shade offered by the covered seating inside the stadium. Although almost dinner time, it still has to be close to ninety out. Too hot to be running around.

"I'm guessing she saw you watching her earlier and is messing with you," John suggests, turning to go back the way they came. A creaking sound makes him turn back.

Sam's head jerks up at the sound of heavy hoofbeats. Before she can react, a large bronco comes barreling down the narrow isle, nostrils flared, the whites of his eyes showing. Snorting loudly, he tosses his head before kicking out and striking the fence. The wood splinters, and the contact pushes the horse into a greater panic as he races toward them.

Grabbing her about the waist, John hauls Sam out of the way while shoving Ally back at the same time. The three of them fall inside the open door of a stable and then watch in disbelief as the horse charges past.

"Whoa there!"

Sam scrambles to her feet, recognizing the voice. Tripping over Ally's leg, she stumbles to the doorway and looks out.

Less than twenty feet away, Ember is on a beautiful brown horse. With unflinching skill, she maneuvers her horse alongside the bronco. Reaching out, she yanks at some sort of strap attached to its stomach, pulling it free. The response is immediate. Tossing its head again, the bronco stops kicking and allows Ember to take ahold of its lead rope. Sliding down from her mount, she then begins to walk both animals back.

Stepping out of the stable, Sam winces when she sees the look on Ember's face. Her green eyes flashing, she's obviously not happy to see them. "What are you kids doing here? Why's this animal out here?"

"We saw someone we know walk over here, and we were just trying to catch up to her," Sam explains. "I'm sorry, we didn't know it was a dangerous area, Ember."

"And you don't need to apologize, Sam," Ember says, her shoulders relaxing. "I was just startled. This horse shouldn't be out here. It certainly shouldn't be here with *this* on it," she adds while holding up a leather strap. "I'll be tracking down his owner and having a long conversation with them."

"What is that?" John asks.

Sam gives John a sideways look. His tone is much harsher than normal for him and it has more to do than being rattled by the horse. She suspects he already knows the answer to his question.

"This," Ember says, giving what looks like a

big leather belt a shake for emphasis, "is what's called a bucking or flank strap. It's used by riders to make the horse buck and it's only applied right before the event. Luckily it has a quick release, so I was able to get off. I was getting Butterscotch ready for our barrel race when I saw you go past and I was going to invite you to come watch."

"Lucky for us you were here," Ally says quietly, still shaken up.

"I wouldn't call any of this lucky." Ember settles the strap over her shoulder and starts walking the horses again. "You kids should go back and enjoy the show. I'll find out how this horse got out here."

Watching Ember walk away, Sam has the distinct feeling the owner isn't going to know what happened to his horse. In spite of the potential danger, the corner of Sam's mouth turns up and she rubs at the goosebumps on her arms. They're getting close.

17

FOLLOW THE LEADER

"She was probably just messing with you, and the horse was a random thing," Hunter offers while throwing another log on the fire.

"Seriously, Hunter?" Sam says, exasperated with her brother. "You really think it was all a coincidence?"

"Oh, sure, Sam." Hunter drops the other log in his hands back on the pile and sits next to John. "Because it makes so much more sense to think that in the two minutes you lost sight of Mallory, she went and found someone's horse, put a bucking strap on him and set him lose on you!"

Sam flinches. She'd walked right into that one.

"He has a point," Ally says quietly.

Cassy pokes at the fire with a long stick. "I agree. None of it makes sense. I wish it did, but it might just be a series of unrelated events, Sam."

Hunter leans out from his spot next to John so he can look at his sister. "Personally, I think it'd be cool if a Banshee really haunted these woods. But a lost valley? That one's a stretch. Even for you."

"Tomorrow, I'm going to talk to Ranger Sparks about those two guys," John interrupts Hunter before the argument can go any further. "I agree that something about them is off, and he'd probably want to know they're wandering around out here. I don't think they're camp guests."

Feeling somewhat vindicated, Sam is relieved to have John's involvement. At least this way Nathan will be alerted to any wrong-doing they might be involved in. They can't do much more than that at this point.

"Who's up for hot chocolate?" Lisa announces, approaching the campfire with a tray of cups. Several sweatshirts are slung over her arms.

Even though it was a scorching hot day, it's cooling off rapidly, which is typical this high up in the mountains, and a slight breeze has picked up. Sam is thankful for her sweatshirt and pulls it on while silently mulling over what her brother said. Could it be that her imagination has gotten the best of her this time?

"Come on," Ally says softly. "It'll be dark in about an hour. Why don't we go take some hot showers before we get ready for bed?"

Cassy leaps to her feet, her own sweatshirt clasped in her hand and a piece of licorice in the other. "Did you say hot shower?"

Laughing, Sam throws her hands up to ward off Cassy's enthusiasm. "Now I know the one thing that'll get your attention faster than food. Which, by the way, I have no idea how you're still eating."

Cassy responds by popping the rest of the candy into her mouth and then takes one of the hot chocolates. "Thank you, Lisa," she says formally. Turning back to Sam and Ally she gives a proper curtsey. "I'll have you know that in some cultures, my iron stomach would be revered."

Sam takes a cup too and then toasts her friend. "When you find that land, fair food princess, I am sure you will rule over it."

Relieved to see that Sam's attitude is still good, Ally giggles at the exchange. Pulling her hoodie on, she picks up Rocky's leash. "Let's take him with us. Just in case of any… owls," she adds with a smile.

By the time they reach the bathrooms, their hot chocolates are almost gone and Cassy has turned her focus from what their midnight snack should be to guessing how many minutes the hot water will last.

"Twenty minutes," Ally says with confidence. "It was fifteen minutes last time, but that was earlier in the day on a Sunday. It's almost eight and the middle of the week so there should be more left."

Sam snaps her flashlight on and off, considering Ally's reasoning. They don't need the light on yet, but it might be getting dark out by the time they walk back. "Twenty-two minutes. And do you think we could bring Rocky in with us, instead of—"

Ally looks up when Sam's voice trails off. "What's—"

Sam puts a hand out in front of Ally to stop her, both from talking and physically. Cassy also stops and looks curiously at Sam. "Look," Sam whispers, pointing beyond the bathrooms.

The three girls stand silently in the twilight and watch as Mallory pauses in the distance, near the trailhead to the waterfall. Sam ushers them off the trail and under the shadow of the trees just before the other girl turns to look furtively around. Apparently not seeing them, she turns back and disappears down the trail.

Sam only hesitates for a moment before setting her mug on the ground and moving again. "Let's follow her."

"Sam!" Ally says, rushing to keep up. "I don't think this is a good idea."

Cassy moans audibly as they pass by the bathrooms and warm showers. "Do I have to point out the *very* obvious flaw to this plan? Hello? Killer bronco and screaming Banshee!"

Sam glances at Cassy and gives her a rueful grin. "Yeah, but why would I want my plans to start making sense?"

Cassy smiles back, and to Ally's frustration, appears to be going along with it. "What do you think she's doing out here? Why don't we just… I dunno, go tell John?" Ally asks.

"We have to go now or we'll lose her," Sam counters. "I think she's going to the same trail as those two men and if we follow her, we might be able to figure out where it goes."

"It's almost dark," Ally presses. "And you know Lisa wouldn't be okay with this."

"She's right," Cassy agrees. "My sister would freak."

At the head of the trail now, Sam can't deny that they're right, and she feels a twinge of guilt. Snapping on the flashlight, she offers a compromise. "Okay, what if we only follow her far enough to see where she's going and we won't go any longer than a half hour? That way we'll be back before it's dark. If she's mixed up with those guys in something, she could be in trouble. This might be our chance to find out what it is, so we can let someone know about it. John could tell Ranger Sparks tomorrow when he talks to him."

Ally chews on her bottom lip.

Sam anxiously looks from her to the trail and back again. They're running out of time.

"Oh, come on," Cassy says, grabbing Ally's hand. "I can handle my sister. How much trouble can we get in for going on a walk before bed?"

Sam doesn't wait to hear the answer, and hurries to lead the way with Rocky in tow. Careful to avoid stepping on branches or anything else that will give them away, she also turns the flashlight off after they've hiked for five minutes. Although murky, there's still enough daylight left to make the trail out well enough without the flashlight. The deer trail is only fifteen minutes or so in and that's where Sam suspects Mallory is headed.

"This is where we ran into Ernest," Ally whispers when they've gone a bit farther in silence. "Did we lose her?"

Sam is about to admit defeat when the distinct sound of a snapping branch up ahead makes them all stop. She puts a hand instinctively on Rocky's head to stop him from barking and he relaxes under her touch.

"There!" Cassy murmurs so quietly that Sam almost doesn't hear her. But she's right. There's a flash of movement just going around the next bend.

Encouraged, the three girls pursue, almost tip-toeing over the dirt and roots. By the time they catch up, they see a couple of branches still moving where Mallory stepped off on the deer trail.

"I knew it!" Sam whispers triumphantly.

"Can we go back now?" Ally asks nervously.

"Just a little farther," Sam pleads.

"We still have a little time before we have to turn back," Cassy offers.

When Ally doesn't argue against it, Sam eagerly charges ahead. The deer trail is barely more than a small swath of trampled-down earth, and it's much harder to see it in the fading light. She's thankful now for the wind, because without the noise it's making through the tree-tops, Mallory would hear them for sure.

The trees quickly become thicker, and the terrain, steeper. Sam finds herself scrambling over larger boulders and across a fallen cedar tree. It doesn't take long before a nervousness settles into the pit of her stomach and she isn't positive they're still on a trail. Stopping on the other side of the log, she leans up against it and looks back at Ally and Cassy. Shaking her head, she holds a hand up to stop them from following. "We should go back."

"Finally!" Ally gasps, her face looking pale in the gathering darkness.

Cassy leans forward to help Sam back over the tree, when a man shouting from somewhere nearby makes them all freeze.

"What are you doing here?"

Sam's breath catches.

"I did what you asked," Mallory's voice is faint, but recognizable. "Now let him go!"

Sam's eyes widen and she looks at Ally, who stares back with as much confusion as she feels. Sam searches the trees to her left, in the direction of the conversation. Sure enough, there's another small trail that Mallory must have taken.

"Wait!" Mallory screams.

A large gust of wind roars through the mountainside, cracking branches high above them, the trees moaning against the force of it. It muffles part of the conversation.

"…coming with us!" a man barks. Mallory screams. The clear sound of a scuffle ensues and then receding movement away from where the girls stand huddled. Rocky begins to growl low in his throat.

"We have to go get help!" Cassy cries.

Sam reaches for the hand Cassy offers and starts to climb back over the log, when Rocky suddenly lunges forward, yanking the leash free from around her wrist. "Rocky!" Sam shouts, spinning back in time to see him leap forward onto the other trail.

"Rocky!" Ally wails, rushing forward to clamber over the log.

"I can't leave him!" Sam turns the flashlight back on and heads after him without even thinking.

Ally pauses, looking back at Cassy. "Go get help," she directs. Taking the big red fabric hair scrunchie from her mop of hair, she turns and quickly loops it over a branch, marking the entrance to the other trail.

Cassy nods, fighting back tears as she watches Ally disappear after Sam and Rocky.

18

THE LOST VALLEY

"Sam!"

Sam sucks in ragged breaths, fighting down her rising panic. She can't find Rocky. Hands on her knees, she stays bent over until Ally catches up and then slowly rises to greet her. "You didn't have to come, too," Sam gasps, still breathless.

Ally throws her arms around her best friend. "I'd never leave you alone out here!"

Sniffling, Sam steps back from the embrace and wipes at her nose. She doesn't know what she'd do without Ally. Pointing the flashlight at the ground, her brows draw together as she's faced with the fact that Rocky might be lost. "I can still see a trail. I'm guessing he must be on it."

"Let's go, then." Ally moves in behind Sam, since the trail is too narrow to walk side-by-side. "Cassy went back to get help."

Sam groans inwardly but doesn't waste any time worrying over the consequences of their nighttime outing. They still have to find Rocky and try to help Mallory.

The trail seems to be following the steep side of the mountain, working its way down into a valley through a series of brutal switchbacks. While going up is of course hard, the descent is even harder on the knees. The fact that there's loose dirt and rocks makes the going even more treacherous.

"Why hasn't he come back?" Ally asks after hiking in silence for several minutes.

Sam shakes her head. "Maybe he caught up to them and they thought he was Mallory's dog and grabbed his leash. Or he got turned around and is just running blindly on the trail in the wrong direction? I should have listened to you, Ally."

"It'll be okay," Ally assures her friend. "We'll find him. He's too smart to get lost for very long."

"Rocky!" Sam calls for what feels like the hundredth time. The frustrating part is that she can't yell his name as loud as she'd like. While there's still plenty of noise from the wind covering up their movement, she can't risk the men hearing her. She has to have faith her loyal friend will find them on his own.

Digging her useless cellphone out from her back pocket, Sam checks the time. Almost nine. Looking up, she frowns at the sky that's rapidly losing its color. As they've descended into the valley, the air has become noticeably cooler and she's thankful for their sweatshirts.

"Look!" Ally urges, tugging on Sam's hood and pulling her up short.

Sure enough, the trail is finally leveling out and up ahead it appears brighter, indicating an opening in the canopy of thick trees around them. Creeping forward cautiously, Sam gasps when the basin comes into full view.

They're standing on a knoll on the edge of a small valley with steep sides all around it. On the far end is a thin waterfall leading to a small stream that meanders through dense foliage and around a large, out-of-place hill in the center of it all. The cooling air has caused a mist to form around its base, lending to the foreboding theme of the girl's plight. Although trees are growing from the hill, the side facing them has been cleared, exposing an obviously man-made rock face, complete with intricate carvings.

"The lost valley," Sam murmurs, in awe of the scene laid out before them.

"You were right," Ally whispers next to Sam. "It looks like someone has been digging here."

"We know who's doing it," Sam corrects Ally. "But something tells me those two guys aren't on their own, and somehow, Mallory has gotten mixed up in it."

Seeing movement on the trail below them, Sam drops down to one knee and pulls Ally down with her. Emerging from the undergrowth and into the open space near the entrance of the mound pyramid is Mallory. Her hair is in disarray, and even from this distance, Sam can tell her eyes are red and wide with fright. Her arms are tied securely behind her back.

Sam is so focused on Mallory that she fails to notice the sounds approaching them until Rocky bounds up over the crest of the trail and nearly knocks them over. Trying desperately to stifle her squeal of joy, Sam sits down hard on her backside and wraps her arms around Rocky's dirty neck. Ally joins them in a group hug there on the ground.

Fighting off her dog's wet kisses, Sam is acutely aware of the danger they're still in. "We have to go," she says to Ally, who doesn't need any further encouragement.

Standing, Sam knows the climb up the switchback in the looming darkness won't be easy. However, they've clearly stumbled onto some sort of illegal operation and Mallory is in trouble. She wonders if she misjudged the girl from the beginning or if she was a part of it all along. It really doesn't matter anymore.

"At least we have proof now," Sam whispers with some relief. "It'll be hard not to believe us when we show them this!"

"I'm afraid you won't be showing this to anyone."

Sam whirls around to find the source of the

voice, and discovers the larger of the two scruffy men blocking the trail. He's holding a shovel like a bat and the implication is clear. Rocky begins to growl again but this time Sam wraps the leash twice around her wrist and holds on tight.

"Ranger Sparks knows where we are," Sam states with a confidence she certainly doesn't feel.

The man's expression clouds and he takes a menacing step forward. "For your sake, I hope you're lying. Now, start walking." He gestures towards the mound pyramid with the shovel. "There's someone who wants to have a talk with you."

19

LESSONS HARD LEARNED

The main room of the mound pyramid lies just inside the entrance and is much larger than Sam expects. Its walls are tapered and appear to have been made from blocks of either carved stone or baked clay. Crude paintings are scattered over its surface, depicting various activities that were likely important to the ancient culture that drew them.

Sam is fascinated by it all, while at the same time frightened of the situation they've gotten into. That *she* got them into. Glancing guiltily at Ally, she pulls her friend in closer. They've been through so much together, but it never seems to get any easier. What if this is the one time they don't figure a way out?

Mallory looks up from where she's sitting in the far corner, and she gasps when she sees them. "What are you doing here?"

Several battery-operated lanterns offer enough light to see things clearly, but Sam doesn't know if that's a good thing or not. Mallory's hands are still tied and her face is tear-streaked. Lying on the ground next to her is Ernest. One of his eyes is swollen shut and his lip is bloodied but Sam has a feeling that if it weren't for being hog-tied, he'd still have plenty of fight left in him.

"Ernest!" Ally cries. "What have they done to you?"

"I'm okay," Ernest barks, doing his best to turn his head so he can see them. "But you'd best be figuring a way out of here."

"Shut up, old man," their captor orders.

"What are *you* doing here?" Sam directs to Mallory, ignoring the man looming behind them. She notices the two are situated next to several box-like contraptions spilling over with dirt. Sam recognizes their construction from the effigy site. They're the same type of devices that the students were using to sift through the dig for artifacts.

"They took Ernest," Mallory replies. "Yesterday, after he confronted Jackson and Curtis and told them to stop what they're doing. I was just trying to get him back."

The man ushering them inside gives Sam a shove from behind when she hesitates too long, and she stumbles forward with a grunt, pulling Ally with her. Rocky growls again.

"I found your friends," Jackson growls.

"They're not my friends!" Mallory shouts at the man, her voice breaking. "Let them go, Jackson. Why did you bring them here? They don't have anything to do with this."

"They do now. Nicely done, Jackson." Professor Tisdale emerges from an opening in the back of the room, carrying a lantern in one hand and a large bag in the other. Tossing the bag at Jackson's feet, he then gestures to the dark cavern behind him. "Go get the rest of it. Our timeline just moved up. Curtis is already back there."

Sam swallows hard. Although she suspected someone on the dig had to be involved, she's still shaken to see the professor. "I don't understand," she says hoarsely. "The effigy is such a big deal for your career. Wouldn't this mound pyramid be even bigger? Like, make you famous?"

Mallory chortles loudly, causing the professor to flinch. "Professor Tisdale is a fraud. He didn't find this *or* the effigy, and none of it's documented. The dig permit was a front to get what he needed up here to illegally move the artifacts through the black market."

"Says the nineteen-year-old, first-year student," Professor Tisdale hisses. "I too was an idealist when I started twenty years ago, but it didn't take long to figure out where the real successes lie. I was going to keep the effigy a legitimate dig and continue to *nurture* my teaching career. But the bureaucracy of the university is preventing even *that* from happening now. The permit will expire at the end of the summer and won't be renewed, thanks to a local preservationist group. Of course, once young Mallory here stumbled onto the operation, I had to change the game plan anyway. But now, that won't work either thanks to you nosy kids."

Shaking his head, the professor tsks loudly while moving closer to Sam and Ally. Pulling aside his jacket to reveal the wooden handle of a pistol, he then looks at them evenly, his face devoid of any emotion. "No, the only way to finally get the lifestyle I desire is to take it for myself, and no one is going to stop me." Tilting his head, he looks beyond Sam and Ally and jerks his chin towards the opening. "Of course, young Mallory is correct to say that I've had some local help."

Sam pivots to look where he's gesturing to discover Mrs. Olivia Barker standing in the entrance to the pyramid, her small figure a dark silhouette until she moves farther into the room.

Gone is the playful disposition of the shop owner as she turns narrowed eyes on Sam and Ally. "Where's the other girl?"

Jackson has retrieved the bag and walks around the professor to carry out his orders, but he pauses and looks nervously from Mrs. Barker to Professor Tisdale. "There are only two of 'em."

Closing her eyes briefly, the older woman's nostrils flare. "No, you fool, there are *three*! We have to go now," she continues, turning back around to leave. "Set the plan in motion, Professor."

Sam doesn't want to know what the plan is, but is afraid they're about to find out.

20

ANCESTRY SECRETS

"Ernest is my grandfather."

Sam didn't think it was possible for anything else Mallory said to surprise her, but she stares back at the girl, open-mouthed. "What?"

The four of them are now sharing the limited space in the corner, with the man named Curtis watching closely. Although smaller than Jackson, he has a cruel mouth and dangerous air about him. The gun he's holding firmly in one hand only reinforces the impression.

Mallory looks down at her feet, splayed out in front of her. "I knew I had a grandfather living in Sanctuary but had never met him. When I heard about the dig, I thought it would be a good opportunity for me to finally meet him."

Ernest clears his throat. "There are a lot of reasons why we never met, but none justifiable," he says with as much dignity as possible. Still hog-tied, he's speaking with his cheek pressed into the dirt. "When Mallory contacted me and asked if I could supply the dig, I knew as soon as I saw her that she was my granddaughter."

"But by then I'd already had my run-in with the professor," Mallory explains. "We'd only been in the campground for a few days when I literally stumbled over a bag with an artifact in it."

Sam glances at Ally. She feels the story is far-fetched, and it's obvious her friend feels the same way.

Mallory rolls her eyes. "Come on. I don't have any reason to be making things up *now*," she implores, shaking her hands still tied behind her back for emphasis. "I really did trip over it. It was a bag with tools and random stuff for the dig, and it all spilled out. When I started putting it back, I found a relic wrapped up. It obviously wasn't from the effigy because we hadn't found anything like that yet. When I asked Professor Tisdale about it, he tried to come up with an excuse. But for a smart guy, he's really bad at thinking on his feet."

Curtis chuckles at this, alerting Sam to the fact he's listening to the conversation.

"What happened?" Ally asks.

"I made it clear I didn't believe him, and he… threatened me. He went from the nice docile teacher to homicidal Indiana Jones in about ten seconds. Tried to tell me it was part of a hush-hush project he'd be announcing soon, and if I breathed a word of it to anyone, he'd have me expelled from the school." Mallory looks pointedly at Sam. "That was the day you heard me in the bathroom. I'm sorry I was so rude, but I really just didn't want you guys to get involved."

"If that's true," Sam counters, "then what about yesterday? We could have been seriously hurt by that horse!"

Mallory hangs her head. "When Ernest didn't meet me when he was supposed to last night, Jackson found me instead and told me that they had him. He said unless I got you guys to follow me there, they'd kill him. I thought I was just a distraction. Honest. I didn't know they were going to do that."

"I'm afraid most of this is my fault," Ernest interrupts. Grunting, he pushes over onto his left shoulder so he can face them better. "After Mallory told me on Sunday that she thought the professor was up to something, I met with Ranger Sparks and the sheriff. I suggested they keep a closer eye on things without giving any specifics."

Sam's brows crease in thought. Sunday. "The meeting he had!" she says to Ally. "That explains why Ranger Sparks told us to stay away."

Ernest tries to nod his head, but grimaces when he only succeeds in rubbing dirt into the cut over his eye. "I told you the Banshee story to try and keep you out of there. If I'd known it would only draw your interest, I would have kept my old mouth shut."

Sam smiles at him, in spite of the situation. "I have a habit of finding enough trouble on my own. I'm sure I still would have managed if you hadn't been involved."

"Maybe so." Ernest coughs and winces, but

takes another ragged breath before continuing. "Today, when I saw our friend Curtis here and Jackson headed for the shop, I put it together. I ran into 'em out there near the dig once and it didn't take much to figure they don't belong around here. But instead of simply going to the sheriff, I had to act the fool and confront 'em. They jumped me a short time later before I had a chance to find Ranger Sparks."

"They're going to frame us," Mallory chokes out, her eyes welling with fresh tears.

"What do you mean?" Ally asks nervously. She looks sideways at Sam.

Professor Tisdale moves up next to Curtis, and with a silent nod, takes over his position. "What she means is that I'll be shocked to discover that my own student was working secretly with her grandfather to loot this ancient mound pyramid. Who better to team up with to track it down than a mountain man who's roamed the area his whole life? Oh, I already submitted a letter of concern to the school yesterday about some of her unacceptable behavior."

Mallory begins to cry again, and Sam's anger

boils over. "You'll never get away with this!"

The professor raises an eyebrow at Sam. "Such spirit, Samantha. It's a shame you got caught up in this."

Sam swallows around the tightening knot in her throat. They know too much. The only reason they're allowing them to see everyone and talk so openly with Ernest and Mallory, is if they have no intention of letting her and Ally leave.

"Ranger Sparks already knows you're up to something, and my friends know about Jackson and Curtis," Sam blurts out, her heart racing now with fear. "They're on their way here right now!"

Professor Tisdale calmly looks at his wristwatch and then taps his foot on the ground. "While I admire your tenacity, your logic is flawed." Removing a pocket knife from his back pocket, he tosses it to Ally. "Release the hogtie strap from Mr. Tucker, Ally, but leave his hands tied and then slide the knife back to me."

Jackson plods into the room then, three bags slung over his shoulders. The bags are bulging with undisclosed items. "We're ready."

Nodding, the professor bends over to retrieve the knife Ally has slid back and then looks pointedly at Sam. "Your friends and Ranger Sparks know just enough to play right into the little scenario I'm creating. It's clear that you and Ally had no idea myself and Mrs. Barker were involved. Stand up." Pulling the gun from his waistband, he points it at them when they don't respond immediately. "Come, now. The one point of accuracy to your claim, Sam, is that we don't have much time. You see, there's a rather dangerous section on the flat top of the pyramid I'd like to show you. Unfortunately, by the time your rescue party gets here, they'll discover you rather foolishly followed Mallory and her grandfather onto it before it collapsed."

"You leave them out of this!" Ernest bellows, making a lunge for the armed man as soon as he gets his feet under him. But injured, hands bound, and still recovering from being tied up for several hours, the older man is no match for the professor, who easily side-steps the attack and follows through with a solid blow to Ernest's back with the butt of the gun.

"Get him up!" the professor yells at Curtis.

Soon, the ill-fated group is led outside. It's nearly dark now with only the outline of the valley visible against the dusky sky. A bright moon has crested the mountains, lending a small amount of light to the dreadful scene being played out.

"Sam," Ally whispers, huddling close to her friend. "What are we going to do?"

Sam's mind races as she struggles to come up with a plan. Mrs. Barker has been left behind at the entrance to the pyramid, standing with several bags that Sam assumes contain priceless artifacts. The four of them are flanked by the professor, Jackson, and Curtis. They're all armed and herding them up the side of the mound pyramid. While the mound is scattered with trees, it's mostly covered with smaller shrubs and foliage, making the going slow.

Time. Sam thinks, looking out at as the floor of the valley gets farther away. "We need to distract them," she whispers back to Ally. "Someone has to be coming soon."

Ahead of them, Jackson is climbing over a fallen tree and it's just the opportunity Sam needs. She can pretend to fall on it and twist an ankle. If they want to throw her into a collapsing mound of mud and clay, they'll have to carry her there!

Her breath coming in short gasps now as her adrenaline surges, Sam prepares to make a loud scene but never gets the chance. As she steps onto the log, there's a sudden flurry of movement to their right, emphasized by cracking and popping branches.

"Hey!" Jackson shouts, turning his gun in the direction of the sounds.

Sam backs away, bumping into Ally. Mallory reaches around them both to grab at Sam's arm. Curtis grunts from behind them when he runs into Ernest, who's also stopped, and his flashlight bobs frantically over the ground around them.

Professor Tisdale, out in front, turns back to see what the commotion is. "Keep moving!" he orders, his face unreadable in the darkness. In response, a deafening wail rises from the same area of trees and is then joined by another, across from it on the other side of them.

Everyone scatters.

Grabbing Ally's hand, with Rocky's leash in her other, Sam turns and runs blindly past Curtis, back down the mound. Not daring to look back, she's aware of Mallory on her other side and can only hope the heavier footsteps behind them is Ernest.

The hair-raising screams continue, circling in behind them and surrounding the three men left behind.

"Keep going!" Ernest grunts when they're enveloped by the woods of the valley floor.

Sam doesn't need any encouragement. Although she's finding it hard to get a full breath, she doesn't stop. Rocky pulls her along, heading for the trail that originally led them into the lost valley. She's acutely aware of Mrs. Barker still standing at the entrance as they approach.

"Hello?" the older woman calls out. "Who's there?"

Slowing, Sam and the others do their best to skirt around the light coming from the lantern Mrs. Barker is holding, but the trees are thicker here and they can't find the trail.

"Stop!" The professor's order is followed by the very distinct sound of a bullet being chambered. As he comes closer, he brings a light with him, but Jackson and Curtis are nowhere to be seen.

"This is insane," Ernest says solemnly,

moving out in front of the girls. "You got what you came for." Pointing towards the bags for emphasis, he then wags his finger at Professor Tisdale. "Take it and go."

The professor shakes his head and takes another step closer. "I'm afraid that isn't possible."

"That's far enough!"

Spinning around, Sam searches out the new voice. A combination of new flashlights and increasing moonlight reveals Ranger Sparks in the clearing behind them. Cassy and John are standing off to one side, while a large man in a sheriff's uniform is on the other. Sam has never seen him before. Both he and Nathan have their weapons drawn and pointed at the professor.

"Put the gun down, Professor," Nathan orders. His dark eyes are unflinching. "It's over."

21

A TRUE SANCTUARY

"I can't believe it's already our last day here," Cassy pouts. Turning over on her pool float, she faces the other three girls floating out on the lake with her.

Sam twirls her hand slowly in the water, thinking back over their time in Sanctuary. It's been three days since their scare at the mound pyramid. She was certain Lisa would cut the trip short and drag them all home but to her surprise, it didn't happen. It had a lot to do with both Ernest and Nathan convincing her how the girls stumbled into the trouble.

"I wish we didn't have to go, either," Sam

says. "It turns out Sanctuary is normally a pretty cool place."

Ally giggles. "I don't know, Sam. I'm sure if we stayed long enough, you'd find us another mystery."

Mallory sits up on her float, dangling her legs in the water to either side. "Grandpa Ernest has invited me to stay with him for the rest of the summer."

"That's great!" Ally says happily. "So everything is straightened out with the school?"

Mallory nods. "The sheriff spoke with the dean personally and explained how I tried to stop Professor Tisdale. They're sending out a team to go over the mound pyramid in a couple of weeks, after they've gone through the proper channels. I'm hoping I can get on the team."

Sam smiles at their new friend. "That's great, Mallory! You'll have to let us know what you discover."

"Come on," Cassy urges, paddling toward shore. "If we stay out here any longer, we'll be crying about our sunburns later tonight, and I plan on a very, very long hot shower."

Sam rolls her eyes, but kicks her feet in the

water to chase after Cassy. "How in the world can you be thinking about a hot shower? It's got to be close to a hundred out here!"

"At least she wasn't talking about a second lunch," Mallory offers, having come to understand Cassy's voracious appetite rather quickly.

"Did someone say lunch?" Hunter swims up alongside the girls as they approach shore.

John splashes his friend and also manages to drench Ally and Sam at the same time. "We just had a picnic, Hunter!"

Ally squeals in response to the cold water, but Sam sits up and straddles the float, swinging around to face the boys. "Oh, it's on!"

Mallory is the first join in on the water fight, but soon all six kids are engaged in a flurry of splashes and yelps. It lasts for a full ten minutes before they drag themselves to shore.

Rocky runs to greet them and heads for Sam first, yapping around her feet until she plops down on her towel and plants a kiss on his nose. Exhausted, she lies back and takes a moment to catch her breath.

"Careful, or you're going to burn," Ember

offers, sitting next to her.

Daenerys runs a circle around Rocky until he leaps to his feet and gives chase. The two tear off through the sand as if they've always been best friends.

"Rocky is going to miss her," Sam says, propping herself up on her elbows.

"You're all welcome to come back to Sanctuary any time," Nathan says, sitting on the other side of Ember.

"I hope we can come back later this summer to see the mound pyramid in the daylight," John says. Ally and Mallory join the group with him while Cassy and Hunter run after them, having gotten left-over hot dogs from Lisa.

"Really, you guys?" Sam says in disbelief, squinting at her brother and Cassy.

Hunter shrugs, his mouth full and Cassy simply grins.

"I wouldn't mind seeing it again under better circumstances," Ally adds, "but I don't know if I'll be able to handle walking through those woods."

"What do you think really happened out there?" John asks. "I mean, we all heard… it."

"It was the protector, of course," Ernest says matter-of-factly.

Sam looks to where he's sitting nearby in the lounge chair Lisa offered him, complete with sun shade. The picnic at the lake was his idea. He showed up in an old truck with a BBQ in the back and a cooler full of food. He said it was his way of thanking them for coming to his and Mallory's rescue.

"The, um… protector?" Ally asks, afraid of the answer.

"But you told us you made up the story of the Banshee," Cassy counters.

Ernest's wrinkled face is hard to read, and he simply tilts his head, inviting someone else to answer.

"He did," Sam confirms. When everyone looks at her, she loses some of her confidence, but scrunching her nose she blurts out what's been on her mind for days. "There might have never really been a Banshee, but the effigy is real. So, maybe the animal protector depicted on it is, too."

"The lynx," Ally whispers.

Sam nods. "According to what I read, the

lynx would have been the guardian of both whoever might have been buried in the effigy… *and* the mound pyramid."

Everyone sits in thoughtful silence for a moment.

"The world is sometimes a place of unexplainable mysteries," Ernest says. "I've found that it's best to simply accept things and move on, else you get too caught up in answers that aren't there."

Sam looks out at the sparkling lake, set against the dramatic backdrop of the rugged cascade mountains. Ernest is right. And she's content without knowing exactly what happened at the pyramid.

Turning to Ally and Cassy, Sam finds both of her friends staring at her, and they all slowly smile at each other. While there might be some unexplainable mysteries, there's plenty that need solving and there's no doubt they'll dig up another one soon!

THE END

Have you read all of the **Samantha Wolf mysteries**? Find them on Tara's author page at Amazon!

Be sure to check out her cozy mysteries featuring Ember Burns in Sanctuary under Tara Meyers on Amazon.

ABOUT THE AUTHOR

Tara Ellis, an Amazon bestselling author, lives in a small rural town in Washington State set in the beautiful Pacific Northwest. She enjoys the quiet lifestyle with her two kids and several dogs. Tara was a firefighter/EMT, and worked in the medical field for many years, before committing herself to writing young adult and middle grade novels full-time.

Visit her author page on Amazon to find all of her books!

Made in the USA
Monee, IL
19 July 2020